# Bewitching the Immortal

## Holiday Immortals Novella Series, Volume 1

Brenda Sparks

Published by Brenda Sparks, 2024.

**Bewitching the Immortal**

~Acknowledgements~

First and foremost, my deep appreciation goes out to my readers. I love you guys!

I must give a special shout-out to Tonya Wilson, without whom Papa Legba would not have made an appearance. Thank you for the inspiration!

To Dr. Rebeca Porter, loads of respect and a huge thank you for your amazing editing.

To my husband, words can never express how grateful I am for your support and assistance. Everything in this story, from the cover to the pages in between has been shaped by you.

And last but most certainly not least, heartfelt gratitude to my loving friends and family, especially Barbara and Dominick. I am so grateful for their support and help in sharing the Holiday Immortals with the world.

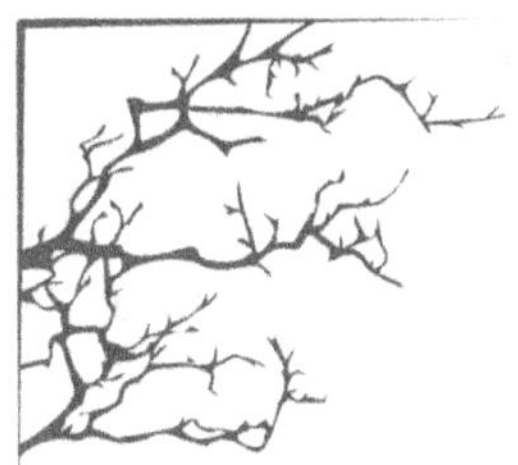

# Chapter 1

Tabetha pulled her cloak tighter about her shoulders bracing against the crisp air. On this All Hallows' Eve, leaves of red, orange, yellow, and brown danced on the wind around her hooded head. Her witch blood thrummed in her veins as if somehow it sensed what was about to happen. A smile took her full, ruby lips when she arrived at her destination.

Tabetha paused a moment to note the three-story home with its wrap-around porch. Normally, the thing beckoned people to sit a spell, but tonight there would be no relaxing. A shiver raced down her spine. Either from the chill in the air or anticipation of tonight's event, she wasn't sure which.

As it had been bespelled to do, the door opened automatically when she approached the stairs to the porch. The delicious scent of incense and potions welcomed her inside. A faint hum in the air mixed with the voices coming from the neighboring room.

"There you are! Greetings, my dear friend. Greetings."

Tabetha unbuttoned the broach at the neck of the cloak and removed it with the usual flair. She tucked it in the closet next to the door then made her way over to her friend.

"Alli, it is great to see you." Tabetha gave her dearest friend, and fellow coven member, a tight squeeze.

"I'm so glad you were able to come to the séance."

"I wouldn't have missed it for the world. Our coven leader made sure we all knew she expected perfect attendance tonight."

Alli shrugged. "Yeah. I got the email too. What can we do? She needs all of our combined power to summon you-know-who."

Alli locked arms with Tabetha and led her into what was normally the living room. Tonight, however, it had been transformed. Where bookcases full of old books normally stood, dark curtains in shades of maroon and black hid the tomes. All furniture had been removed. A carpet with a large Hecate's wheel symbol lay in the middle of the hardwood floor. On its edges, creating perfect circles, a variety of pillows were placed in two rows. A grouping of candles created an inner circle around the symbol. Their soft yellow-orange glow cast strange shadows about the room.

"Wow! I love what you've done with the place." Tabetha winked, knowing her friend had just yesterday complained about the work it took to get ready for tonight.

"I know, right? You'd think it was Halloween or something, and we were getting ready for a séance." Alli rolled her eyes.

Tabetha gave her friend's hand a squeeze before untangling their arms. "Seriously, it actually look great. We shouldn't have any trouble conjuring Legba."

"From your lips to the leader's ears." Alli chuckled. "She came by no less than five times this past week to check on things and make sure they were just right."

"That's because tonight has to be perfect." Hestaba sauntered up to the pair. Her black dress swirled around her legs; each step accented with a sharp tattoo of her stiletto boots on the hardwood.

Alli and Tabetha immediately straightened and nodded their heads in an expected show of reverence and greeting.

"Tonight *will* be perfect, High Priestess," Tabetha assured their leader. "It must be. Everything is riding on getting help from Legba."

"You have that right, my dear. With all the covens preparing for the potion competition on the winter solstice, we need to ensure Legba chooses to bless us rather than the other covens. Our potions must be stronger and work better than everyone else's if we are to win. And you know, we won't be the only coven contacting Legba."

Alli's eyes widened. "That reminds me. I ran into a member of the Shadow Warlock Coven at our apothecary."

"Ugh! The S.W.C. Sorry to hear that. They are so full of themselves. They are the worst."

"No, it's actually a good thing. He mentioned they discovered an old tome in a member's attic. Apparently, it contains some amazing spells, at least that is what he claimed. He bragged about how, with this tome, their coven couldn't lose this year."

The high priestess crossed her arms over her chest and huffed. "We'll see about that. All the old potions in the world can't compare with potions blessed by Papa Legba. Speaking of," Hestaba raised her arms in the air and turned in the direction of the majority of the coven. "The time has come. Let us alight on our cushions and begin."

A hushed murmur hummed through the crowd. The witches did as instructed, each choosing a pillow on the séance carpet. Only the soft rustling of fabric carried on the air as the last of the coven took their seats.

When everyone stilled, an unnatural hush fell over the room. For the second time that night, a shiver raced along Tabetha's spine. She drew in a deep fortifying breath before letting out a slow exhale.

"Everybody join hands," instructed the priestess. "Now I will lead the séance, but we all need to combine our magic. The stronger we make the call, the better the chance Papa Legba will hear our summons and come to us. Is everyone ready?"

Tabetha joined Hestaba in glancing throughout the room. A sea of heads bobbed up and down. Peace settled over Tabetha. These were her people. These women could be trusted with her life. They would always have her back. Unlike some of the other covens in the area, theirs was a tight group. Their leader might be a little strict, but she only did so when necessary, such as demanding they all be here tonight to work together to ensure their success when their lives would be on the line.

One by one, the members closed their eyes in concentration. Tabetha rolled her shoulders then closed her own eyes to call her magic. It flowed from the earth, through the home and pillow, up her legs. The tingling pooled in her belly for a brief moment before ascending to the core of her power, her heart. The magical energy vibrated Tabetha's body.

"Clasp hands. I'm ready to begin," instructed Hestaba.

Tabetha grabbed Alli's hand first. It was hot, hurt to hold, but Tabetha managed to hang on. She knew Alli's magic came from the element fire, so it was no surprise when it manifested, the witch's flesh heated. The other hand she grabbed wet her palm. If she didn't know better, she'd think it was perspiration, but Tabetha understood Bea's power came from the element of water.

All sensations from the two hands disappeared when her own magic flared to life. It sent electric current down both arms to join forces with the elements next to her. Each witch in turn did the same until all their elements combined into a singular thrumming.

Tabetha opened her eyelids in time to catch Hestaba's eyes opening unnaturally wide. They appeared opaque, like the eyes of the dead. In a raspy voice, she called, "We, the witches of the Enchanted Midnight Coven, summon Papa Legba on this, the most holiest of days, All Hallows' Eve. Papa Legba, come to us, we beseech you. Come, so we may present you our offering and speak with you."

A gentle wind blew the flames of the candles. The shadows grew longer, more ominous. Several of the witches trembled. Alli's grip on Tabetha's hand tightened, painfully so. Anticipation flowed through the group, the trepidation of the coven feeding one another's fear.

But Legba did not come. Frustration replaced trepidation as the coven waited on bated breath for the man of the hour to arrive.

*That's just like a man*, thought Tabetha. *Figures he won't show. He's probably busy giving another coven his blessing.*

"Papa Legba, we, the witches of the Enchanted Midnight Coven, summon you on this, the most holiest of days, All Hallows' Eve." The priestess repeated. "Come, so we may present you our offering and speak with you."

Tabetha closed her eyes again in concentration. She summoned the earth, drawing from it every newton of power she could handle. She pushed the energy out to the collective, hoping it would provide the boost they needed for the summoning. Her effort rocked her body like a magnitude-seven earthquake. The hands she held slid, and Tabetha tightened her grip to keep their circle unbroken.

A fierce wind whipped through the room. Tabetha's long, blonde curls beat her face, obscuring her sight when she opened her eyes to see what was happening. A powerful blast of energy hit the circles.

"Hold tight," Hestaba screamed over the rushing wind and electric hum of energy. "Don't let go of the person next to you. Don't break the circle."

The group began chanting the ancient call to Papa Legba. The women swayed; the inner circle going in one direction, the outer going in the opposite. Their chant grew in strength with each repeated chorus until it nearly drowned out the howl of the fierce wind whipping about the room. Tabetha pulled more magic from the earth, hoping it might be enough to keep their circle intact.

An unseen force choked the flames of all the candles at once. Darkness engulfed the room. An unsettling quiet lay thickly over them as the wind died alongside their voices.

The hair on Tabatha's neck rose first, but the fine hair on her arms wasn't far behind. Tabetha blinked furiously, trying to clear her vision. Knowing she couldn't let go of the hands she held without the spell breaking, she tossed her head to remove her tresses from her eyes.

As her vision adjusted to the full moon's light streaming through the window, a figure emerged. In place of where the candles had once sat, a male now stood. Long legs encased in dark pants led to a small waist. The black leather vest he wore opened over a bare torso that sported a six-pack with two well-defined pecs. His face had a strong jaw. The skull makeup on the upper half of his face made his black eyes seem both menacing and yet fascinating, like dark pools that beckoned. His top hat sat upon his braided hair, the beads in which jangled when he moved.

A cocky, half grin took Legba's handsome face. "So, I was summoned dis year, by a group of witches?"

Hestaba swallowed as if finding her voice. "We would like your help if you are inclined to give it, Papa Legba."

Legba nodded his head. His top hat remained perfectly in place as if held there by magic.

"What is it dat a woman as beautiful as yourself needs my help with, *mon cher*?" Legba purred in a Cajun accent as he squatted down in front of the priestess.

Hestaba cleared her throat. "We wish to have your blessing. We have a potion and spell competition coming up. We will be going against the best covens."

Legba straightened to his full height. "Is your magic not good enough to win on your own?"

"No, no," Hestaba assured hastily. "It is. Our magic is powerful."

Legba turned and locked eyes with Tabetha. She seemed to fall into their black depths. She felt lightheaded, unsure if it was the expended magic or his eyes that made her feint. She steeled her spine to keep from leaning forward.

"*Oui, cher*. I feel your magic. 'Tis strong with *some* of your coven." Legba's attention returned to the coven priestess. "So why then do you need my blessing?"

"We need it to ensure our victory. There is a rumor another coven may have found a tome that will allow them to cheat. We want to compensate for that with a blessing from you."

"A blessing to allow a fair competition then?" Legba pinned Hestaba with a knowing stare. "You sure you aren't looking for a leg up on the competition?"

Hestaba shook her head with a ferocity that almost had Tabetha believing her lie about the other coven.

Almost.

"We just want a fair fight. Our potions and spells are good. I'd put my coven up against anyone in a fair fight."

Legba nodded. "Very well. You have my blessing. Now what do *I* get in return?"

Hestaba stood. "You can have your pick of anyone in my coven to be your lover tonight while you are on this plane."

Legba cocked his head. "And your members agree to dis?"

Hestaba steeled her features. "They do."

Legba locked eyes with Tabetha. She fought the urge to run. She hadn't agreed to be offered as any sacrifice. Perhaps she'd missed that revelation by being the last to arrive tonight.

Legba slowly turned, perusing each coven member until he again faced Hestaba. A knowing smile pulled one corner of his lips. "Then I choose you, as coven leader."

Relief flooded Tabetha. Hestaba had a much different reaction. Shock widened her eyes, but acceptance immediately followed. The priestess composed herself, nodded her chin in agreement, then slowly took the extended hand Legba presented.

After pulling her to her feet, the couple's forms wavered. As they became translucent, they merged until they disappeared entirely.

"What do we do now?" Tabetha asked Alli.

With a shrug, one of Tabetha's least favorite people, a witch known as Belladonna, offered, "I guess we go home."

Her sarcastic tone grated Tabetha's nerves. Tabetha had never really liked Bella. The two had attended school together, and every chance she got, Bella would get Tabetha in trouble. Tabetha had always been a little better at magic, and Bella loved to use Tabetha's gift to get her in trouble at school. She'd been all too happy when they graduated, and she believed she'd rarely need to see Bella again. But fate had other plans. Living up to her name, Belladonna now worked in the coven's apothecary, so Tabetha had no choice but to interact with her often.

"Home. What a novel idea. Why didn't I think of that?" Tabetha teased.

Bella's eyes narrowed into an intense glare.

Alli nodded. "Actually, Bella has the right idea. No doubt you will be busy tomorrow. With the competition just a few weeks away, I'm sure you'll get a lot of business in the apothecary with everyone needing to practice their potions and spells."

Belladonna stood and tightened her lace shawl around her shoulders in a bracing hug. "You can count on it. We've stocked up on supplies for months anticipating the competition. Our coven isn't the only one that is practicing."

Alli, being the second to the high priestess, cleared her throat and murmured a spell to illuminate the room with electric light. When she spoke, her voice soared on the air, loud and clear for all to hear. "Congratulations, witches! We did what our dear High Priestess asked of us. By combining our magic, we were able to show Papa Legba we are worthy of his blessing. Our priestess has become the sacrifice to ensure the blessing. We must do her proud by winning the competition." Muttered agreement flowed through the crowd. "To that end, we will practice our potions and spells. Bella and Hestaba have worked to make sure the apothecary is well-stocked and has everything we need. Find time every day from now until the contest to hone your magic. You can never practice too much."

A cheer rose from the crowd in comradery. The energy created by the group's excitement permeated the space. Tabetha's blood bubbled with excitement as if her magic couldn't wait to be tested. Tomorrow, her first stop would be the apothecary for supplies, then she would spend the entire weekend working on her potions. It would be vital to have a life-saving potion on hand during the competition. After all, one never knew just what kinds of deadly potions or spells the other covens would bring to the contest. Coven members were so tied to each other, every loss was felt by the entire coven. The stakes couldn't be higher.

Tabetha glanced around the space, noting the happiness and excitement on the faces, and knew a moment of trepidation. She hoped those bright eyes and wide smiles didn't turn into death masks.

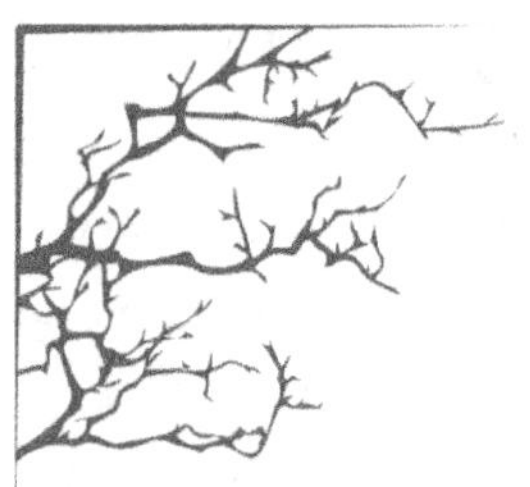

# Chapter 2

Azrael burst into the room, dressed in his usual reaping attire of leather from head to toe. He carried his scythe in one hand and a coat draped across the other arm. Nothing said the Grim Reaper has come for you like a pair of shit-kicker boots and a shirt-pants combo the color of midnight. All the man needed was a skull for a head instead of the flesh and bone he actually sported, but that skull-for-a-face thing was just something the humans made up to go along with the whole death-has-come-for-you thing.

"Let's go, old man," the Grim Reaper called out, laying down his scythe to shrug into the long, leather duster with silver buckles that completed his attire.

Father Time pinned the reaper with a hard stare. "You know I hate it when you call me that. I may be eons old, but I hardly look a day over fifty."

True that. The male Azrael had called friend for so many centuries he'd lost count, could easily pass for a human in his late forties what with those slight wrinkles around the eyes and graying hairs on his head. At least he was still fit. But then it was almost impossible for an immortal not to be. After all, most of them only aged for so long, then never grew any older looking. Their bodies didn't age either. Yep, as immortality went, spending it in a body that was in great shape and a face that never aged, wasn't the worse way to go through existence. Although lately, Azrael had wanted a little more out of life than just reaping the souls of the dying and escorting them to the afterlife. He wanted something new, something he'd never experienced before. But after living for several epochs there wasn't much that fit into that category.

Azrael finished buckling his coat and cracked his neck by wrenching it to each side with the palm of one hand.

Pakiž ran a hand over his short, graying beard. "What do you want? I was enjoying a peaceful afternoon of reading."

"Sorry to interrupt your solitude. You seem awfully comfy on the sofa there in front of the fire." Azrael crossed the room to warm his hands by the flames. The heat danced over his skin in the most delicious way, reminding him of the place most souls would rather not go to.

"Unfortunately, I need a favor. I've got a pending death, and the Fates are all busy, so I need you to pitch hit for me. It shouldn't take long. Just the standard take-the-last-of-their-time-so-I-can-reap-their-soul deal."

Pakiž sighed as he placed a bookmark in the novel, closed the book, and pushed off the couch to stand. "If no one else is able to go with you to reap that soul, I am happy to help."

Azrael crossed back to grab his scythe while Pakiž donned the jacket to his gray suit. "I appreciate that. Sorry, but you are the only one available. We should go. Let's not keep the woman waiting."

Pakiž grabbed his own scythe and touched the reaper's arm. Being the Grim Reaper meant it was up to Azrael to locate the dead, for it was he who knew instinctively where the soon to be deceased was. His subconscious homed in on the dying woman. It created an ethereal thread for him to follow to her location on the human plane of existence.

Pakiž's hand gripped Azrael's forearm. As Azrael coalesced his form, Pakiž's molecules melded with his. Azrael raced along the thread. In less than a second, the two re-formed as separate beings in a warm room. Both remained incorporeal as was their standard operating procedure, since one never knew exactly what you'd find at a death scene. After all, he could reap while either solid or incorporeal, so there was no need to be seen by anyone still alive near the dead person.

Azrael opened his eyes to a light amber glow from the embers in the fireplace that warmed the bottom of a black cauldron, the steam from which rose thickly into the chimney. His gaze roamed the wall, noticing the vines creeping up to strings of lights strung from the exposed beams in the ceiling. The view from the open windows along with the pitch of the ceiling into an A-frame, told him they were most likely in an attic that had been converted into a bedroom. His gaze traveled along one of the green vines. It led down to a large bookcase on which many old, leather books were stacked next to several potted plants. It stood next to a round bedside table which hosted a half-drank glass of greenish liquid.

Azrael took a deep breath. The scent of earth and incense overwhelmed him. It was a heady combination.

"Such a shame." Pakiž tsked. "It always saddens me when we have to reap one so young."

Azrael's eyes wandered to the bed. Upon it lay a young woman. Her thick, blonde curls splayed over the pillows. The dress she wore, with its mystic leaf, pinecone, and mushroom pattern, had a high slit up one side, giving him a tantalizing view of her long leg. The view didn't disappoint higher either, thanks to the V-neck that dropped practically to her navel. But it was her beauty that struck him like an arrow to the heart.

Even in death, the woman seemed the picture of health. Her pale skin still retained a radiant glow. A small nose was the perfect complement to her sculpted cheekbones and beautiful blue eyes. Unlike his friend's shade of blue, which was more ice than ocean, her eyes were the color of the sky on a bright summer day.

Pakiž voiced the exact thought going through Azrael's mind. "What the heck happened to her? There is no sign of trauma or injury. She looks like she should be able to get up off the bed and go dancing."

Azrael nodded. "I agree. It is so strange. It won't be long now until she takes her last breath, and we can find out some answers."

A gurgle sounded from the back of her throat. Her bosom sunk as the last of her breath left her body.

"Now." Azrael readied his scythe, gripping it tightly in both hands. "Do the honors, Father Time."

Pakiž's grip on his own scythe tightened. He extended his hand toward the dying woman and began calling the last of her time to him. It flowed from her body in otherworldly tendrils that glowed with the effervescence of a thousand suns into his scythe.

With the remainder of her time absorbed, Azrael approached the bed and extended his scythe. An ethereal hand rose from the flesh to touch the blade. Azrael then used the scythe to draw the soul from the woman's body.

Once free of the physical world, the woman's soul looked down on her fleshy form. A frown pulled the corners of her mouth. And for the first time in all the eons he'd been reaping, Azrael wanted to pull the deceased into his arms and kiss the frown off her face.

*Whoa! Where the hell did that come from?* Azrael willed the inappropriate thoughts away. He was a professional after all. It was time for the next step.

"Hello, love. Welcome to the afterlife," Azrael greeted with what he hoped would be a warm smile.

"Afterlife?" The woman glanced from her body, to Azrael, to Pakiž, and back to her body. "Am I...am I dead?"

"I'm afraid so." Pakiž nodded. "But don't worry. Azrael is here to answer all your questions and take you to the afterlife."

"But I don't want to be dead." The woman's eyes squinted in grief and disbelief.

Azrael laid a hand on her shoulder and gave it a comforting squeeze. "No one does, love. But when it is your time, it is your time."

The woman's eyes narrowed in suspicion. "Who are you?"

Azrael placed his free hand over his heart. While holding onto his scythe, he bowed deeply at the waist.

"Allow me to introduce myself and my friend." Azrael straightened before continuing. "This is Father Time, and I am the Grim Reaper."

"But you can call us Pakiž and Azrael." With a smile, Pakiž pointed first to himself then to his friend. "And what might your name be?"

"I'm Tabetha, but people sometimes call me Beth."

*Tabetha. Tabetha.* Azrael tried the name on for size. It was the perfect name for the perfect woman.

*What the...another intrusive thought!* What was up with him today?

Tabetha locked eyes with him, pulling Azrael from his reverie. "Father Time? The Grim Reaper? You're real?"

"Yes love, we are real, as real as two immortal beings can be."

"So, I'm really dead? How? How did it happen? What killed me?"

"We were wondering that too." Pakiž shifted his scythe to his other hand.

"Do you remember anything?" Azrael asked, his curiosity piqued.

Tabetha's soul began to pace. "Not really. Let's see. I was at the apothecary." She glanced at her body and shook her head. "No. Wait...Obviously, I was home. I...I can't remember."

Pakiž cocked his head. "Is it typical for people not to remember how they died, Azrael?"

The reaper shook his head. "No. Usually, people remember exactly what happened."

Tabetha stopped pacing and crossed her arms around her waist in a bracing hug. "So, what does that mean?"

"It may mean nothing. I honestly don't know." Azrael wished he could offer her answers that brought more comfort. He preferred to reassure the dead. It made the transition easier.

"Look, I need to be getting back. I have lots to do and taking part in a reaping wasn't on the list." Pakiž smiled at Azrael. "But when a friend calls, you answer."

Azrael nodded. "Go. I can take things from here."

Tabetha placed both hands on her hips. "What exactly do you mean by that?"

"I leave you in the very capable hands of Azrael." Pakiž's glance shifted from Tabetha to Azrael. "Good luck!"

Before Azrael replied, Pakiž dematerialized.

"Where'd he g—" Tabetha shook her head violently, sending her golden tresses swirling around her shoulders. "No, never mind. I don't want to know after all."

Tabetha moved in front of the fire. She trembled slightly as if cold, which Azrael knew was impossible. "The fire is dying, but I'm not sure if it will burn out before all the potion boils out of the cauldron."

Azrael's form solidified as he stepped beside her and removed the cauldron from its kettle stand, placing it on the brick hearth. "Now there's nothing to worry about."

Tabetha smiled at Azrael as he ghosted back into the form that would allow him to reap her soul. "Thank you. At least my home won't burn down."

"Your home will be fine. We should probably get going."

"Go where?"

"To the afterlife."

That made Tabetha face him. "What is that like?"

Azrael shrugged, making the leather from his duster creak. "It is different for everyone. Your idea of the afterlife is exactly what you will experience. So, tell me, what did you expect?"

"Well, I'm a witch. Our literature tells us the physical body is just a host for the soul. After we die, our soul travels to the realm of Summerland. I believe Summerland is an amazing place with resplendent lands, rivers, and enchanted forests. There we can be reunited with loved ones, reflect on our lives, and even be reincarnated if we wish to try life again."

An ember flew from the dying fire as if it spit the last of its breath. The spark passed through the witch's soul and landed in the shadow on the floor. It rolled up to the head of the shadow.

*Head? What?* A chill raced up the Grim Reaper's spine. *That can't be! Souls don't have shadows.*

Azrael's gaze raked the floor in disbelief, seeking an explanation. Finding none, he scanned the room, determined to find the cause, but though impossible, the shadow came from Tabetha's soul.

Just as he opened his mouth to mention the oddity, Tabetha's form solidified. The next second, the beautiful witch's body wavered and faded until it was once again ethereal. If he'd blinked at the wrong time, he'd have missed it.

Surprise widened Azrael's eyes, and his mouth gaped open. "How did you do that?"

"Do what?" asked Tabetha.

"Become solid?" His heart raced.

"I do not know what you are talking about."

"You were solid. I saw you become solid. Ordinarily, souls can't do that."

Tabetha shrugged, and both eyebrows jacked up onto her forehead. "Maybe I'm not an ordinary soul."

"Perhaps you aren't." Azrael rubbed his chin thoughtfully before he continued, ticking each point off on a finger as he listed them. "You can't remember how you died. You are a witch. You just became corporeal. I think you are very special indeed."

After a thoughtful pause, during which he eyed this amazing soul, he continued. "I think we better go."

"Are you taking me to Summerland?"

Azrael shook his hair, scattering his raven bangs about his forehead. "No. I can't reap your soul if you can turn corporeal. I'm going to have to take you somewhere other than the afterlife."

Tabetha fisted her hands on her hips as her deep blue eyes flared slightly. "If we aren't going to Summerland, where are we going then?"

As much as he knew he shouldn't, there was no other choice.

Azrael pursed his lips together. "I'm taking you to the land of the immortals."

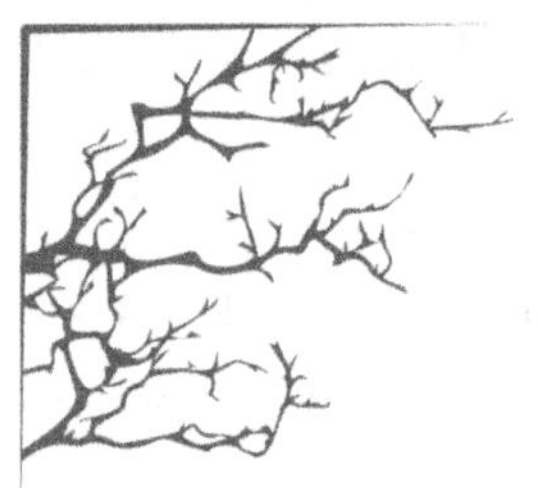

# Chapter 3

The queasiness in Tabetha's stomach eased as her molecules reformed alongside Azrael. When her vision cleared, she glanced around the space. They stood in the middle of a large foyer. The walls of the room were ornate, with black wallpaper sporting a gray damask print. Light streamed through the clerestory windows in dual layers that filled the wall in front of a black circular stairwell. Tabetha's gaze moved from the beautiful architecture to the large circular table in the middle of the space with an elaborate flower arrangement.

*Funny,* she thought. *Azrael doesn't seem like the flower type of guy.*

Of course, he also didn't seem like the type of guy who would have dark parquet flooring with a medallion inlay either, but that is exactly what they were standing on. What did fit were the shades of black and gray throughout the space. Yeah, that's exactly what she would expect in the Grim Reaper's home.

"Like what you see?" The sound of Azrael's deep voice pulled her from the perusal.

Tabetha's eyes flew to the male beside her. His presence filled the room. He stood at least a head and a half taller than her five-foot-eight frame. Blue-black hair was swept to the side of his face with a shake of his head. The leather coat he wore, buckled across his broad chest, boasted a fit physique. The patrician features of his handsome face conveyed knowledge and wisdom far beyond her young years. His dark eyes were lit with a passion for life as he stared down at her.

Hadn't he asked her something? A question? Her brain struggled to get back with the program and off the male with the warrior's face, one the Goddess could have sculpted herself.

"Um, yeah. Nice place you have here." Tabetha gave him what she hoped would be a convincing smile.

"I'm glad you like it." Azrael's arm extended in a right-this-way gesture. "Let's go into the living room so we can discuss why I brought you here."

"About that. You mentioned I'm not normal. What do you mean?" Tabetha followed her host into the next room.

The room carried on the foyer's dark themes. Windows, nearly the length of the wall, lined opposite sides of the space. The light pouring in from the curtainless structures created shadows about the room that made the black paint on the walls and ornate molding appear to be various shades. A large painting of the four apocalypses riding magnificent steeds hung above the fireplace with its ornately carved mantle. On each side of the structure, two dark burgundy chairs sat welcoming them.

Tabetha accepted their offer and alighted on the fancier of the two. "Quite the place you have here."

Azrael shrugged out of his coat and laid it over the back of the couch, facing the fireplace. "Mind if I change into something a little more comfortable?"

Tabetha's mind couldn't help but appreciate the suggestive nature of that question. Although, she figured she probably shouldn't bring mortal context to his realm.

"Of course," she encouraged, secretly anticipating what his ideas of more comfortable might be. After all, she wasn't exactly a virgin. Her coven encouraged connections, and sex was one of the easiest ways to connect and share energy.

Azrael snapped his fingers and instantly new clothes replaced the black reaping outfit. He wore a white dress shirt, unbuttoned halfway down his muscular chest, exposing the trail of fine hair that led south. His dark hair lay slicked back from the chiseled features of his face. His broad chest tapered to a narrow waist. The shirt and black jeans he wore left no doubt that under the material there was a hard, muscular form. Tabetha nibbled her top lip to keep from licking her lips.

He sat in the chair on the opposite side of the fireplace. "Tabetha, we need to talk about what happened."

"What do you mean?"

"I've already told you that you are different than any other soul I have reaped, but you need to understand exactly what that means."

When he hesitated as if trying to find just the right words, Tabetha spoke. "Go on. You don't need to sugarcoat anything. I'm dead for goddess's sake. How much worse can things get?"

"You are brave, I'll give you that. Most people in your situation would be freaking out, I'd imagine."

"How did others handle being brought here?"

"They didn't."

"What do you mean?"

"No one else has ever been brought here." Azrael shook his head back and forth slowly. "Not one."

"No one?" Tabetha allowed the disbelief to ring in her tone. Surely, she wasn't the first.

"You are the first person I've brought here, because you are the first person I've ever tried to reap whose soul turned solid," Azrael confirmed her unspoken question. "In all the eons I have been a reaper, never have I failed to carry out my duty by escorting someone to the afterlife. At least, not until today."

As if on cue, Tabetha's form solidified, and her hand flew to her mouth. "Why can I turn solid?"

The grim scrubbed a hand over his face. "I wish I knew. Why don't you tell me everything you remember prior to your death."

Tabetha placed her hand in her lap and worried the material of her skirt through her fingers. "Okay. How far back should I go? Do you want me to start at the beginning?"

"Yes, the more I know, the better the chance of figuring out just what is going on."

"Okay. I was born twenty-eight years ago to wonderful parents. They were kind and loving."

"Are you their only child?"

"Yes. My childhood was normal. Well, as normal as it could be, given both of my parents were magical."

"Were they powerful?" Azrael eyes flared slightly.

Tabetha shrugged. "I don't really know. They were always doing magic around the house, using it to do the most mundane of chores. I don't know if they were exactly powerful, but they sure used it a lot. At least until the accident."

"Accident?" Azrael prompted, leaning forward to rest his forearms on his knees.

"My parents died in a car accident when I was fifteen. After that, I went to live with my friend, Alli. Alli's parents were friends of my parents. They were all in the same coven."

Memories pushed in on Tabetha. The loss of her parents still stung, and she guessed it always would. To this day, she loved them dearly and grieved them fiercely. She missed their guidance. They had shared very little about witchcraft in the fifteen years they'd been a family, but she didn't blame them. No doubt, they assumed they had plenty of time to tell her what being a witch was all about. They surely believed they had time to teach her all about their ancestors and how to properly channel her magic to create complex potions.

"Potions!" Her gaze locked with Azrael's dark eyes. "I was creating a potion when I died."

Azrael leaned back, rested his elbows on the arms of the chair, and steepled his fingers. "Now we might be getting somewhere. Think back. What potion? Why were you making it?"

Tabetha closed her eyes in concentration and racked her memory. Images of the apothecary her coven owned flooded her mind. She watched Bella hand her various herbs and vials of liquids. After she purchased the ingredients, she stopped by Alli's house for a cup of tea on her way home. Blackness suddenly filled her mind's eye. Just as quickly as the images had come, they disappeared.

Tabetha opened her eyes and scrubbed a hand over her scalp in frustration. "I'm sorry, I don't remember much."

"That's okay. Just tell me what you do remember." Azrael gave her a weak smile.

"Shortly before I died, I was buying items from the coven's apothecary. Then I had tea with my best friend."

"Could either of them have something to do with your death?"

"I doubt it. Alli and I are as close as sisters. The salesperson at the apothecary isn't the nicest person in the world, but we aren't enemies or anything."

"Was there anyone else at the apothecary?"

Tabetha scanned her limited memories. "I don't think so."

"Is it normal to be the only one in the apothecary? Seems like it would be a busy place."

A shiver raced through Tabetha, and she crossed her arms around her waist in a protective hug. "You're right. I always remember it as being busy, but my last time there, I can't remember anyone else being there. What does that mean?"

Azrael narrowed his eyes. "I'm not sure. But we will figure it out."

Tabetha's form wavered and became ethereal. She raised her hands and twisted them back and forth, marveling how the floor was visible through the digits. "Why do I keep phasing in and out? Is it because I was murdered?"

Azrael's hand dropped to his lap as he shrugged. "I am not sure why this is happening to you. But you aren't the first murdered person I've reaped. Perhaps your magic, combined with your desire to know who killed you, is why your soul struggles to remain in the physical world."

"So do you think if I figure out who killed me, my soul can rest?"

"Maybe. I'd like you to stay here with me while we figure out what is going on with your soul."

Stay here? With this sexy, mysterious male? Tabetha could think of worse places to be. He was temptation incarnate. And if he wanted to help her figure out who killed her, all the better. But he was *waaaay* too serious. The thought of spending goddess knows how long in his stoic presence gave her pause. A plan formed. If only she could use her magic in this form.

Her form shimmered and turned corporeal. She turned her hands over to be sure she could no longer see through them.

*Perfect timing,* she thought.

"Okay. I'll stay. But we need to do something about the accommodations."

"What do you mean? I thought you liked my home."

"Well, to be truthful, it is a bit dark for my taste," Tabatha said, glancing around. "I know. I'll just make a few minor adjustments."

Before he could protest, Tabetha drew on her magic and imagined the room in shades of light pink. Magic coursed through her feet, up her body, and out the arms that formed a letter T. Her witchcraft flew from her fingertips to paint the room in her Pepto Bismol vision.

Azrael jumped to his feet as a sea of pink coated the walls, carpet, and furniture.

"There. That's better." Tabetha crossed her arms over her chest.

"I should say not." Azrael turned a full three-sixty and snapped his fingers.

Immediately, the room regressed to its previous state. Tabetha raised one eyebrow and pursed her lips. So, the reaper's magic could be used on more than just himself. Well, two magical creatures could play this game.

"Then how about this?" Tabetha sent her magic out to create new decor.

The room filled with her vision of rainbow walls, green furniture, and yellow candles in the fireplace. This time, she even changed the portrait above the mantle to a unicorn and made clouds dance on the ceiling.

The effeminate gasp from Azrael's mouth brought an image of him clutching pearls to mind. A smile took Tabetha's face.

"I...You...I..." Azrael stammered in shock.

"Or perhaps something like this."

Tabetha changed the room again, this time making it circus-like, complete with red and white striped walls and a dirt floor. The couch turned into an elephant. Its trumpet nearly deafened Tabetha, but the look on Azrael's face was worth the temporary discomfort.

Like a fish out of water, Azrael's mouth opened and closed repeatedly. No sound escaped save a small squeak.

"What's the matter?" Unable to contain herself any longer, a hardy laugh burst through Tabetha's lips. "Don't you like it?"

Azrael pulled his horrified stare away from the circus tent walls. His dark eyes locked with hers. Tabetha registered the exact moment he realized she teased him. His expression softened. He opened his mouth again, but this time he threw his head back and a deep chuckle burst from his lungs.

"You got me," he exclaimed when at last he gained enough composure to speak. "I can't tell you the last time someone pranked me."

Tabetha smiled, enjoying the amusement on his handsome face. "It is good to see you laugh. You don't have to be serious all the time."

Azrael snapped his fingers, returning the room to its gothic aesthetic. "It feels good to laugh. My job is a serious one, literally life and death. You have reminded me what it is like to be carefree."

Azrael crossed the room in two long strides and placed a hand on Tabetha's cheek. The contact sent an electric jolt through her. The sensation warmed her blood, sent heat pooling low in her belly.

"Thank you...Tabetha suddenly seems too formal. May I call you Beth?"

"No one other than my family has ever called me Beth."

"Is that a no then?"

Tabetha rested her hand over his. "I think you calling me Beth is perfect."

Tabetha's form wavered. Azrael's hand fell through her ethereal features, and bereavement settled on Tabetha at the loss of his touch.

"I'm sorry," she said as Azrael stepped back.

"No reason to apologize. You can't control the phasing."

"Maybe once we figure out who killed me, I'll be able to control it."

A sadness overtook Azrael's face. "Maybe. Or maybe once we figure out who killed you, you'll be incorporeal forever."

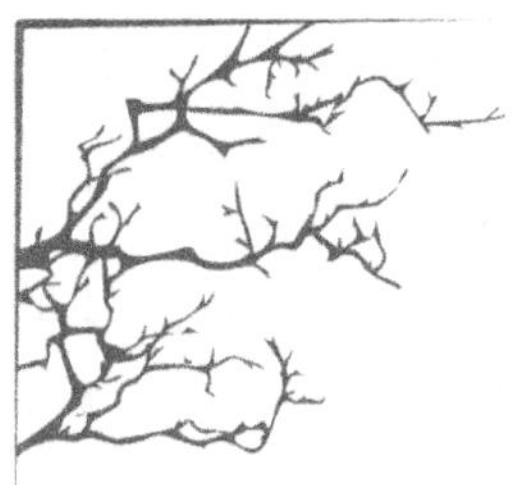

# Chapter 4

Azrael's vision blurred the expansive space as he raised a cup to his mouth and took a long drink of ambrosia. The sweet nectar of the gods flowed down his throat to tickle his belly in what should have been the most delightful way. However, today, he didn't enjoy the small pleasure. No, today, like every day over the past two months, concern furrowed his brows, and thoughts of the beautiful woman asleep upstairs filled his mind.

The days had melded into looooooong weeks. Each day began with him sharing a meal with Beth, at least when she was corporeal. Over their meal, they would relive the moments leading up to her death. They discussed the possibilities ad nauseam to no avail. Yet, they were no closer to discovering who had killed her.

Azrael banged his fist on the table. The sound of fine China tinkling brought a sigh from across the room. His gaze locked on the beauty standing in the doorway.

"I see you are solid this morning."

"I woke up this way." Beth ran a hand down the front of her flowy dress.

Azrael rose and held a chair for her at the table. "Please sit. I made you something to eat."

Beth glided across the tile floor and graced him with a straight, wide smile as she placed her perfect bottom in the seat. "Thank you. I realize I've said this before, but you really are a great host."

Azrael sat in the chair next to her. "I have tried to make your stay as comfortable as possible."

"You have," she assured him, enthusiastically nodding her head as she pinched a bite-size morsel off the strawberry muffin he had made especially for her, knowing it was her favorite flavor. She made quick work of the nugget before she continued. "You have been very kind. Much more than I expected."

"Did you expect me to be an ass?" Azrael cocked one eyebrow and gave her a smirk.

Beth lowered her eyes to the table and chewed her bottom lip between her teeth. "Honestly, I did not know what to expect. You are the Grim Reaper after all. Your reputation preceded you."

"What reputation? I wasn't aware I had one."

"Well, perhaps not a reputation, per se, but humans have certain beliefs about the Grim Reaper."

"Such as?" he prompted before taking another sip of his ambrosia.

"Well for starters, you are supposed to have a skull for your face."

Azrael joined Beth in a chuckle. "I have no idea how that rumor started, probably a painter who was frightened to die."

"You're probably right." A blush rosied Beth's cheeks. "I'm glad they got that wrong, by the way."

A cocky grin raised one corner of Azrael's mouth. "Really? Why exactly are you glad?"

"I don't know," Beth took a sip of Azrael's ambrosia before popping another bite of muffin in her kissable mouth as if stalling for time, hoping he'd let it drop.

He wasn't letting her off that easy. This hottie had teased and tortured him for weeks. She ghosted around his home, tempting him with those full ruby lips and eyes that begged him to touch her.

"I think you know." He leaned in her direction and took her hand in his, rubbing her wrist with his thumb. "I think you know exactly why you are glad I don't have a skull for a face."

He watched her swallow. As her delicate throat worked, his thoughts went to kissing the creamy column. She was the embodiment of seduction, and it made his desire want to stand up and say hello. Had she been someone other than a soul who he'd tried to reap, he'd have had her in his bed by now. But as it was, he'd felt decorum was the better part of valor where this amazing creature was concerned. Of course, that didn't stop his libido from raring its head from time to time, like now.

"I admit, it is nice to have a handsome face to see rather than a scary skull," Beth confessed.

"Handsome?" Azrael's mouth became the Sahara.

He noticed the way her pulse quickened under his thumb. Could she be as attracted to him as he was to her? Maybe his self-imposed celibacy was for naught.

Azrael pulled himself up by the short hairs.

*Stop it! You can't go there,* he thought.

He needed to change the subject and quick. Luckily, he knew just the topic to be safe. "Let's go over your passing. Maybe you'll remember something new."

Beth blew an exasperated sigh. "We do this every day. I never come up with anything that helps us figure out who killed me."

Azrael nodded his head and gave her hand a squeeze. "I know. I know, but perhaps today will be different."

Beth blew a loud raspberry and rolled her eyes. Azrael couldn't help but find it charming. He chuckled.

"Appease me. Come on. Let's just go through it again."

"Fiiiine." Beth's frustration came through loud and clear. She snatched the last of the muffin from the plate with her free hand and popped it between her lips as if she needed the fortification to endure going through the events once more.

"We begin with the possible suspects."

"Then move on to motive, opportunity, and means. Yeah. I know."

Beth pulled her hand from his and crossed her arms over her chest in a defiant stance.

As her warmth diminished, loss settled on Azrael. "The first suspect is Alli. She was the last person you recall being with prior to your death."

Beth shook her head.

"First, she's my best friend." She counted each point on a finger as she rattled them off with perfunctory ease. "Second, she is like a sister to me. Third, she has no motive."

"I agree. From what you've shared with me previously, she had opportunity, but no motive." Azrael lifted the carafe from the table and poured Beth a cup of coffee as she whispered her thanks. "How about the clerk from the apothecary? What was her name? Nightshade?"

As Beth reached for her coffee, the ridiculous pun had the exact effect Azrael hoped it would. Beth's laugh bubbled up from her belly and an explosion of pure joy overtook her delicate features. The light in her eyes danced in the most mesmerizing way.

"You mean Belladonna? Nightshade. Ha! You were close."

"Yes, Belladonna. What about her? She certainly had opportunity by selling you the herbs for the potion that killed you. And she had means since she could have slipped the wrong herb into your bag."

"She also could have put a poison on the herbs themselves, knowing I would be trying the potions on myself."

Azrael nodded. "Means and opportunity, we just need a motive."

"I can't come up with one." Beth cradled the steaming mug between her delicate fingers.

"Did you two get along?"

"We weren't friends, but then again, we didn't hate each other." Beth took a long sip of coffee. Azrael tracked the mug as it rose to be cradled between her full lips, wishing like hell he was that cup.

Azrael pushed away the thought as he cleared his throat. "Didn't you say, you had some trouble with her when the two of you were in school together?"

"Yeah, but that was a long time ago."

"Any chance she is still holding a grudge?"

Beth placed the mug back on the table. "Maybe, but I can't figure out why she would be?"

"Okay, we'll put a pin in that one for now and come back. Who else did you have contact with right before your death?"

Beth shook her head, sending her golden curls bouncing on her shoulders. "No one."

"Concentrate. There must have been others in the apothecary. Try describing the apothecary and see if it triggers anything."

Beth closed her eyes in concentration. "The apothecary was warm like always. Lots of incense too that smelled like coming home."

"You mentioned before the apothecary was filled with the scent of incense. Maybe if we light a bit of the stuff, the smell will strengthen your memory."

Her eyes popped open, and a full grin drew his attention once again to those juicy lips. "Great idea!"

Azrael raced to the living room and grabbed the incense burner he kept on the table next to the couch. A quick whiff assured him sandalwood filled the burner. He hoped it would be close enough to trigger Beth's memories.

Returning to find Beth staring across the kitchen, he made quick work of lighting the incense. After placing it on the table, he used his hand to waft the wisp of smoke in her direction.

"Mmmmmm. Sandalwood. My favorite."

"Does it smell like the apothecary?"

"A little."

"Try to remember the day you bought your herbs to practice your potions."

Beth closed her eyes once more as Azrael continued to walk her through the scene.

"It's early November. Your coven has just contacted Papa Legba. He's agreed to give the coven his blessing."

"Because of the sacrifice made by Hestaba." Beth's eyes flew open and locked on Azrael. "Hestaba!"

"Hestaba?" Azrael crossed an ankle to rest on the opposite knee.

"Yeah. Hestaba, my coven's high priestess. She is like a second mother to all of us in the coven."

"What did you remember about her?"

"She was there in the apothecary. I remember, now. Hestaba and Bella were with me in the shop. Hestaba and I were both there picking up ingredients to practice making potions...for the contest!" Excitement made Tabetha lean forward in her chair. "The covens were having a contest. I'd been practicing making healing potions for weeks. I'd perfected them and shared the news with Hestaba."

"So, this Hestaba had opportunity. Does she also have a motive?"

"I don't believe so. She seemed thrilled I was practicing for the contest and asked me to meet her at the apothecary to review my recipe. While we were there, she asked permission to share my recipe with the rest of the coven, but I didn't want to."

"Why not?" Azrael prompted, as he added a helping of fresh fruit to Beth's plate.

"Because we witches are very protective of our potions, especially those created by our ancestors. I offered to make a lot to share during the contest. That way, I could protect the coven without giving away my family secrets."

"Seems like a good solution. Was Hestaba grateful?"

"Oh yes. She seemed thrilled. While we were at the apothecary, she made sure I had all the ingredients I needed, even made Bella go in the storeroom for more at one point. She also bought me some rather expensive herbs when I told her I didn't have enough money to get the supplies for both the healing and the life-extending potions."

Azrael leaned back in his chair and rested his forearm on the table. "She sounds like a good leader, doing what she needs to in order for her coven members to be safe."

"After Alli and I had tea, I took the herbs home to make my great-grandmother's recipe from her book of spells."

"Good. Go on."

"Everything went well, as it always does." Beth stabbed a piece of cantaloupe with her fork and pointed it in Azrael's direction. "My magic has never failed me."

"I have noticed that."

"Wait! I remember." Beth put her fork down with such excitement the clink it made against the plate nearly echoed in the kitchen. "I remember! I know exactly what killed me. It wasn't just any old potion."

At last, new information. The excitement bubbling in his blood pushed Azrael to the edge of his seat. "That's great. What was it?"

"I was making a life-extending elixir."

"Shouldn't it have prolonged your life not ended it?"

"Exactly!"

Confusion furrowed Azrael's forehead pulling his dark eyebrows down over his eyes. "I don't understand."

"Don't you see? I drank the elixir. The potion killed me."

"So, you did something wrong?"

"My family and I have made the potion a hundred times over the years. My great grandmother perfected the recipe and passed it down. No one, including me, has altered it. I made it perfectly."

"So then, how did it kill you?"

"If it killed me, there can only be one explanation. Someone tampered with the ingredients I used."

"We seem to have three viable candidates for that: Hestaba, Belladonna, and Alli."

Beth shook her head. "I disagree. None of them have motive."

Azrael steepled his fingers. "I'll agree your friend, Alli, probably isn't the murderer, but I'll reserve my opinions on Belladonna and Hestaba. We need more information on those two."

"Okay, but how will we get it?" Beth tapped her finger on her chin.

Azrael tracked her long red nail as it beat against her plump lips. Lips he longed to kiss. As the thought of kissing Beth sent an electric jolt to the area between his thighs, he reminded himself it would be inappropriate. Inexcusable. She was a soul. He, a reaper. It was not permitted to be intimate with a reaped soul.

The proverbial little devil on his shoulder popped up to tempt him. *She isn't really a reaped soul, is she?* After all, the very fact she was here to tantalize him proved this was no typical reaper-soul situation. Could they? Should he? No doubt her kiss would taste delicious.

"Legba!" Beth's shout pulled him from his reverie.

*Damn.* Nothing kicked a male in his libido like hearing another man's name on a woman's lips.

"Legba? What about him? Don't tell me he was in the apothecary too."

"No, he wasn't. We summoned him during a séance the Halloween before I died. He and Hestaba left together from the summoning. I believe they slept together. Maybe he knows something that might clear Hestaba."

"Or perhaps he will know something that will tell us who the murderer is," Azrael muttered behind the hand resting over his mouth and chin.

Tabetha's form wavered and faded to a ghostly representation of herself. She blew out an exasperated breath. "So much for eating. I wish my soul would stop phasing in and out."

Azrael shrugged. "I know it is frustrating. Let's focus on finding your killer. The rest will sort itself out."

Beth nodded. "All right. Too bad we don't know where to find Legba."

Azrael smiled. "Oh, don't we? He just happens to live in this immortal realm."

Beth's excitement pushed her forward. "Really? No way! Can we find out where he is?"

"I can do you one better. I'll take you to his place right now."

Azrael stood and offered his hand to Beth out of instinct. When she paused rather than take it, he let it drop, wishing like hell that she could control the shifting.

Beth's form rose, then ghosted across the kitchen and through the closed door. When he didn't follow immediately, she popped just her head back through the door to say with a smile, "You coming or what?"

Azrael threw back his head and laughed. "Yes, ma'am."

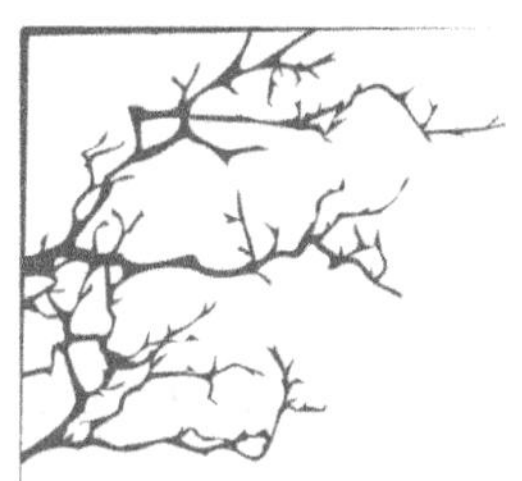

# Chapter 5

A loud knock on the door startled Legba from his midday nap. Nothing bothered a godlike immortal quite as much as not getting his beauty sleep. He rose from the bed, his body stiff as a board like Bela Lugosi doing his best Dracula impression. Yeah, it was dramatic and for no one else's amusement but his, but hey, when one was as ancient as he, he'd take his fun where he could get it. Which was why he spent so much time with witches. They were a riotously good time. Always doing spells and mixing potions that did all kinds of fun and interesting things. They were quite amusing.

As his feet hit the carpeted floor in his bedroom, his quick strides took him across the room. Grabbing his top hat from the dresser on his way out the door, he used his magic to place it perfectly upon the braids on his head. As he made his way through his expansive mansion, he pulled on the lace cuffs of his shirt sleeves and tucked the white fabric into his dark gray pants. Legba wiped the sleep from his eyes and noted his decor as he moved through the hall. Everywhere he looked gilded crown molding and wainscoting shined brightly against the perfect white plaster walls and marble floor tiles. His place could have been featured in the latest issue of *Lifestyles of the Godly and Famous*-if such a magazine existed.

A deep chuckle sounded from his throat as he reached the door. When another round of knocking began, he threw the door open wide.

"What?" he demanded. He softened his voice when he registered his visitors. "Oh, 'tis you Azrael."

His gaze alighted on the ethereal woman next to him. "And I see you brought a friend."

The reaper, dressed in his usual black attire, looking more like he was ready for a motorcycle ride than a friendly visit, nodded. "Hi, Legba. We'd like to speak with you if you have a few minutes."

Curiosity made Legba's right eyebrow shoot up. "The Grim Reaper shows up on my doorstep with a ghost, wanting to talk to me? How can I not oblige?"

Legba stepped aside and ushered them in with a grand sweep of his arm. "By all means. Come. Come. On bated breath, I wait to hear what you have to say."

Azrael, having gone to Legba's home many times in the past, wasted no time leading the trio into the living room. He sat heavily on the velvet couch while Legba joined the party on a matching chaise. The ghost sat as well, next to Azrael, which Legba found rather curious. This wasn't his first ghost, after all. But it was the first one he'd ever seen sit as if it were still human. And that wasn't the only thing unique about this specter. It seemed familiar.

But he couldn't quite place it.

Azrael crossed his leather-clad legs in a manly stance and leaned back against the couch, throwing an arm along the back that settled behind the ghost. The spirit smiled at the reaper, a smile that triggered Legba's memory.

"You are the witch dat summoned me last Hallows' Eve."

Her beautiful eyes locked with his. "You recognize me?"

Legba nodded. "I do."

"But *I* didn't summon you. It was my coven, or more correctly, our leader Hestaba, who summoned you."

Legba rested his elbows on the arms of the chair and steepled his fingers. "No, *cher*. 'Twas you. *Your* magic was what summoned me. Your magic is powerful, yes?"

Shaking her head, the spirit glanced between Legba and Azrael as if uneasy. "I'm sorry, but you are mistaken. I was there, but only to lend my magic to the coven."

"I try not to argue with a beautiful woman, but well, let us just agree to disagree for now." Legba tilted his head in consideration as his gaze roamed over her delicate features. "Tell me your name, child."

Azrael cleared his throat. The glare coming from the reaper would have quelled a lesser being. "Her name is Tabetha, and we've come here for a purpose. I'd like to get back to that if you don't mind."

Well now, this was interesting. After eons of dealing with witches trying to one-up each other, Legba recognized jealousy when he saw it. Here was a grim possessive of a ghost. Legba vowed to probe further.

"I don't mind at all. Do tell, why you have come to my home today." Legba settled back in his chair and crossed his legs to place one ankle on the opposite knee, mirroring Azrael's posture.

Azrael took a deep breath and let it out slowly before beginning his tale. The grim talked with his hands as much as his mouth. Legba listened intently as the reaper regaled him with a story of witches, contests, and the reaping of a soul that couldn't be reaped.

At least not yet.

When he finished, it was Legba who took a deep, steadying breath before speaking. The tale was a lot to take in. He'd never heard of a soul that could cast a shadow, much less become corporeal. This Tabetha was quite a unique witch indeed. Although given her powerful magic, he guessed he really shouldn't be all that surprised.

"So, let me sum up." Legba's eyes narrowed in concentration. "You can't send Tabetha to da afterlife until you can stabilize her soul. You don't tink you can stabilize her soul until you figure out who killed her. You can't figure out who killed her, because she can't remember the details surrounding her demise. And you come to me, why?"

Tabetha leaned in his direction. "We came to you because I remembered Hestaba was a potential suspect. Since you know Hestaba, we hoped you might be able to tell us something that would help us to be able to rule her out—"

"Or in," Azrael added.

"—as a suspect," the pretty little witch finished and worried her bottom lip between her ghostly teeth.

It was quite cute. Legba had to admit he could almost see what Azrael found so fascinating about the woman.

Almost.

The fact she was a soul that needed to get to the afterlife could not be overlooked. That needed to be the ultimate goal here. A soul should not spend eternity roaming around the immortal, or for that matter, human plane.

"So, do you remember Hestaba?" Tabetha prompted, pulling Legba from his thoughts.

"*Oui, cher*. I know Hestaba. I know her well." A sly smirk took his face as his time with the witch played in his mind's eye.

She was a wildcat in bed. Never a dull moment with that one. And wow, how many, many wild moments they had shared over the past months.

"Excellent." Azrael placed an elbow on the back of the sofa and rested his temple against his fist. "What can you tell us about the woman?"

"I not one to kiss and tell," Legba said in a thick Cajun accent as a wide smile stretched the features of his face.

Tabetha waved a hand. "No, no. That's not what we mean. I know she came to you and, um...came as a sacrifice."

Legba nodded. "She initially did, but she and I have been seeing each other ever since. I am not a one-night stand."

Shock widened Tabetha's eyes, and her eyebrow shot up on her head. "Wait. You've been seeing her all this time."

Legba nodded once. "Yes, I visit her regularly on the human plane."

That seemed to grab Azrael's attention. He clapped his hands. "So, you know her well."

"I know her intimately, *oui*."

"Tell us all about her. Has she said or done anything that would make you believe she had a part in Tabetha's death?"

Legba replayed his stint with the coven leader. Most of their time together had been between the sheets, where more moaning than talking had been done. In the few conversations the two had shared, Tabetha had never once come up, at least as far as he could remember. And now that he paused to contemplate it, that seemed a bit strange. Usually, a coven leader would brag about their strongest member, but the only person Hestaba had ever bragged about was herself.

The Vodou god rubbed his chin thoughtfully before answering. "I'm sorry, but I cannot tink of anything she said or did dat would involve your or anyone else's murder."

Twin expressions of disappointment took the faces of the two sitting on the couch.

Tabetha was the next to speak. "I really thought you might be able to help us. We have narrowed down who may have killed me to three suspects. All three are in my coven, so when Azrael said he knew you and you knew Hestaba, I hoped you might be privy to information about who killed me."

Tabetha's form shivered and blurred. Suddenly, the woman sat whole on his couch. Whole! As in no longer see-through. As in no longer a ghost. Every bit as solid as he or Azrael. Shock widened Legba's eyes and made his jaw slack.

Before he could form a single question about the event, Azrael interjected, "Yeah. She can turn solid."

"You could have led with dat," Legba admonished.

Azrael shook his head. "Didn't seem important."

"Didn't seem important?" Legba didn't keep the incredulousness from the tone in his voice. "Are you insane? Have you ever known a soul to do dat before?"

Azrael shook his head, and his eyes softened. "Never. She is very special."

Tabetha cleared her throat. "She's right here. You don't have to talk over me."

Legba blinked his eyes in rapid succession, but her image remained solid. It wasn't an illusion. "Tabetha, you are truly amazing. I knew you were powerful, but I had no idea."

Tabetha crossed her legs and placed her hands in her lap. "You keep saying I'm powerful. Do you think my magic might be a reason why I keep turning solid?"

Legba placed his hands in a position of surrender and shrugged. "I have no idea. What do you tink?"

"We don't know either. We have a theory that if she can figure out who killed her, perhaps her soul will be able to rest, and it will remain ethereal, so she can go to the afterlife." Azrael rested a hand on Tabetha's shoulder and gave it a squeeze. "So, you can see why we need to figure out who killed her."

Legba nodded. "I understand. 'Tis hard to believe, but yes, I understand."

Tabetha worried the material of her dress between her fingers. "So, will you help me?"

"Yes, child. I want to help you. Unfortunately, I don't remember anyting dat would help you to figure out who killed you."

"Then you will visit Hestaba again. Pump her for information." Azrael's tone booked no argument.

Legba met the dark eyes of his friend, his desperation plain to see in their depths. Legba couldn't help but be moved. Between his friend and the witch's unique situation, he was fascinated and determined to help them. It happened to be an added plus that the coven leader wasn't a bad lay either. Win-win they called it. "Absolutely. I will go to her and see what I can find out."

"Oh, thank you," Tabetha gushed. "Thank you!"

The woman rose and lunged into Legba's arms, giving him a hug. When his arms automatically circled around her back, a low, possessive growl of warning came from across the room. Legba immediately let go. Tabetha stood to her full height, and Legba's eyes met the other male in the room. The Grim Reaper's deadly stare bore a hole into Legba's skull, the glare so fierce it practically pierced his brain. That male had it bad for this little witch.

*Too bad they can never be together*, thought Legba. *But such is the way of tings.*

"We better go," Azrael bit out between clenched teeth as he rose and took Tabetha by the hand.

Legba gave his friend a knowing smile. "I tink dat is wise."

Tabetha's gaze flickered between the two as if trying to understand the sudden tension in the air. Legba wondered how the little witch could not realize Azrael desired her. Not only that, but apparently, he didn't want another male interacting with her. That could only mean one thing: he'd developed feelings for the poor soul.

Legba followed the couple to the front of the home and opened the door for them. Tabetha moved through the opening first without letting go of Azrael's hand.

Once outside, Tabetha stopped and turned back to Legba. "I appreciate your help. Thank you, Papa Legba."

Legba bowed his head. "I am happy to do it. I shall be in touch."

"Yes. Thank you." Azrael nodded. "I apologize for earlier."

"No worries. 'Tis already forgotten."

Azrael gave him a weak smile, then turned and led Tabetha in the direction of his home. As Legba watched the pair walk off into the distance hand in hand, he couldn't help but think they had a rocky future ahead of them. He didn't envy that male.

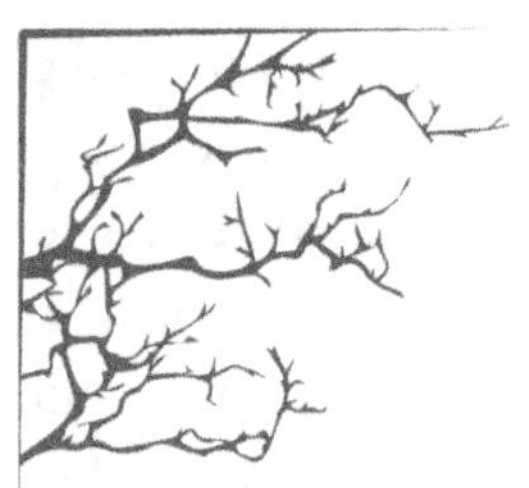

# Chapter 6

Their hands grasped tight as if bound by a love magic binding spell, Tabetha pulled Azrael into his home. Excitement bubbled in her veins. Maybe Papa Legba would come through for her. She shook off any doubts. No maybe about it. Of course, he would. He was Papa Legba after all, and she was a child of his chosen coven.

"Why are you so happy?" Azrael asked. "Not that I'm complaining. You have the most resplendent smile."

Heat crept into her cheeks. "Thank you."

The smolder on Azrael's face made the heat pool low in her belly. The two of them had been flirting since the night they met, the tension building between them. And it had become too much to bear. The will-they-won't-they? The innuendoes and double entendres. The butterflies that rarely left when she was in his presence.

Enough was enough, Tabetha decided.

"So why are you happy?"

"Because I believe in Papa Legba. He will help us."

"Legba is an asset for sure."

"I hope he will be able to pump Hestaba for information."

"Oh, he'll be pumping her all right." Azrael gave a suggestive leer, both eyebrows hopping on his forehead. "I just hope she has information on Bella. I still believe she is the most likely candidate. She had the stronger opportunity and means."

Tabetha shook her head and shrugged a shoulder. "I'm not sold on Bella. I honestly don't have any idea who would have hated me enough to kill me."

A shiver of unease went through Tabatha as she pondered a hatred intense enough to kill.

As if sensing her discomfort, Azrael squeezed her hand. "Let's change the subject. How about we talk about us?"

"Us?" Tabetha swallowed.

Azrael led Tabetha up the spiral stairs toward the second floor, talking as they ascended. "Us. You and me."

He glanced over his shoulder as they rose. His tapered, raven hair fell over his brow, shadowing his eyes. The seduction in his dark gaze heated her core and made passion race through her blood.

"It is time we got to know each other a little better." Azrael turned back around. "If you are amenable to that."

Amenable? Try hot to trot. Core on fire. Need burning within. Yeah, she was ready, but playing coy might be more fun. Make him work for it a bit. Or perhaps instead, she would make him beg.

Tabetha put on a burst of speed and bound up the remaining stairs, tugging Azrael along for the ride.

"Come on, slowpoke." She pulled his arm.

"Where are you taking me?"

"To my room." Tabatha announced.

It was her turn to turn on the smolder and glance over her shoulder. Azrael's eyes darkened with passion. "Your room? I'm intrigued. Whatever shall we do in there?"

As they arrived at the door to her room, Beth pulled her magic and used it to fling the opening wide. "Come inside and find out," she teased. "If you dare."

"Oh, I dare." Azrael smiled down at her.

"That's what I hoped you'd say."

She drank in the sight of him like a woman dying of thirst, savoring every drop. Her finger trailed down the pert, long nose which sat above his lips, lips that were full, held slightly apart as if he waited on bated breath to see what happened next. He had a powerful, rounded jaw. But the most striking feature on his face—those amazing black eyes. They could hypnotize a woman, draw you in, make you lose yourself in their gaze.

The black shirt and jeans he wore covered his body like a glove, outlining his muscular frame. His thick pecs pushed at the material, and she wanted desperately to touch them. Beth trailed a finger down the length of his chest, along the side of his waist, and down one of his muscular thighs.

His hand snaked out, reaching for hers, as if to stop her. Beth threw out a silent binding spell, and both hands clamped to his side.

"Ah,ah, ah," she admonished, wagging a finger in his direction. "It's my time to play."

A half-smile raised one corner of his lips. "Fine, little witch. Let's play. I'm all yours. Do with me as you will."

"Oh, I will. I'll have you down on your knees, panting in no time."

"Promises, promises," His eyes darkened as if he dared her to come through.

Well, challenge accepted.

Her fingers walked down the fabric of his shirt, exposing a little of his flesh at a time as she undid each button one by one. A tantalizing striptease, which hardened his body and sent an answering rush of moisture to her core. Tabetha's mouth watered for a taste of him. Her heated gaze roamed every exposed inch, memorizing each nuance.

Her hunger rose. He was deliciously hard behind those tight jeans. His hips jumped when her eyes landed on his zipper. It shot her into a spiral of need. She recalled her magic to unbind his arms, allowing him freedom of movement.

She was rewarded by him raising a hand to cup her cheek. He lowered his lips to hers. Their tongues danced between their mouths in a waltz as old as time. *Make that a tango*, her mind amended as he deepened the kiss, and their combined desire erupted.

Done with the teasing, Tabetha magicked the offending clothes off both their bodies. Surprise made Azrael break the kiss. When he pulled away, Tabetha brought a hand to her kiss-swollen lips.

"You little minx," her lover teased.

"If you wish, I could put our clothes back on." Tabetha pouted.

Azrael ran a thumb over her bottom lip. "Oh no. They would only get in the way, I'm afraid."

He ran the pads of his fingers lightly over her flesh, blazing a trail from her belly button to the underside of one breast. His hand cupped the creamy mound, kneaded it with loving fingers. Beth stirred beneath the palm.

She scissored her legs, seeking to ease the sensation building there. Her body burned with need, need he created by his touch. Desire poured through her veins like hot lava.

Azrael sucked her nipple into the warmth of his mouth, swirling his tongue over the pebbling bud. It puckered, seeking the sensuous sensation of the moist cavern.

Her fingers fisted in his dark hair and laced in the silky strands to hold him to her in desperation. He drove her body higher, sending her reaching for the precipice with his ministrations.

"I need—" The sensation overloaded her brain, making it difficult to concentrate.

"You need what?" he prompted.

"M-more," she stuttered.

Azrael obliged, sliding two fingers into her wet channel. His thumb found her tiny bud, making circles while his fingers glided in and out. She pushed against his hand, shamelessly seeking his touch.

Azrael leaned back to gaze down her body as his hands kneaded, then caught her nipples between the pads of his fingers and thumbs to pinch them lightly. Beth arched her back hard, the pleasurable pain pushing her over the edge, wringing the climax from her as she covered his hands with her own.

His shaft, hard as steel, pulsed and throbbed against her thigh, looking for an opportunity. To her surprise, he ruthlessly denied it, choosing instead to take her mouth in a punishing kiss. The sensation of his flesh against hers seemed to nearly push him over the edge of restraint. Luckily, he refused to give into the demands of his body, instead seeking to draw her pleasure out.

His fingers slipped out from under hers. Tabetha moaned her displeasure. But a startled gasp quieted the protest when he lifted her into his arms and took her mouth in a passionate kiss as his long strides took them to the bed.

He placed her down, cradling her head on the pillow as her blonde hair clouded around the satin pillowcase. His hand caressed her cheek before he trailed one finger down her body as he walked along the side of the mattress. He knelt at her feet and spread her legs wide before settling between them. He stared at her sex.

"I want to taste you," he growled.

Beth moaned in anticipation.

Azrael draped her legs over his shoulders. He went in to her core, his lips to her, his caress sending her to heaven. His mouth closed over her sensitive nub, sucking it into the warmth of his hot mouth. Beth covered her breasts with her hands, squeezing them in time with his licks.

Azrael suckled her, feeding from her as a dying man inhaling his last meal. Beth thrust her hips against him in wanton abandonment. She breathed his name, the sound a pleading need as her hand found his head. She held him to her, encouraging him to increase the pace. He could do no other than oblige the invitation. Azrael set a furious pace, the action drawing a long moan from Beth. Her head twisted on the pillow from side to side.

He pushed a finger into her feminine core, twisting it while his tongue went back to kiss her nub. She groaned. Her body clamped around his finger. He withdrew, inserting two instead and pushed her over the cliff of ecstasy into a release that surely would shatter her corporeal form—except it didn't, thank the Fates.

She lay panting. Her hard breaths thrust her breasts in delicious invitation. Holding her legs to his shoulders, he edged up her body to take one of the fleshy globes between his lips. His tongue swirled around the peak, drawing tiny circles around her nipple.

"Azrael!" Tabetha fisted both hands in his hair, desperate with the need to feel him inside her.

Instead of giving her what she wanted, his lips blazed a fiery trail of kisses upward to close on the delicate skin of her throat. Azrael crawled over her body, the feel of his flesh against her chest an added pleasure.

His shaft jumped against her core in response. Azrael grasped the thickness in one hand and pushed the tip inside her slick opening. His breath caught in his throat as he slid his steel through the velvety folds. Expecting to be impaled in one hard thrust, Beth instead watched Azrael push slowly inside. She savored the way her body wrapped around his tip to fist him in a wet, tight grip. She convulsed around the mushroomed head, needing more. He glided home. Inch by luscious inch he filled her, stretching her, until she milked his length.

Tabetha arched, and he gradually withdrew. Her core clenched around him, the contact adding another sinuous pleasure. She moaned.

Innnnn.

Ouuuuut.

Each plunge and withdrawal tantalizingly slow.

Azrael braced his weight on his hands. His hips pistoned gently as she floated above the earth. Her calves squeezed his ears. Azrael lowered his firm physique until her flexible, naked form crushed beneath his. Her legs still over his shoulders allowed him to be seated fully within her. Looking deep into his eyes, she watched his pleasure build with each long thrust.

A guttural growl escaped the back of his throat as his thick member slid inside in a long silken glide. She threaded her arms around him, holding him to her, riding his powerful thrusts. Tabetha inhaled, breathing his exotic scent deep into her lungs. It drove her hunger. Half-crazed by desire, she lifted her head to find his lips.

Their mouths locked in a passionate kiss. She poured all her desire for him into the kiss. Their tongues dueled with a ravenous intensity that had them thrusting deeply between their lips. The tension built inside her, deep and full, increasing with every lunging thrust. Her legs dropped from his shoulders to circle his waist, changing the internal pressure.

She came again, screaming into his mouth. Maddened, she released his lips and buried her face in the curve of his jaw. As she nipped and suckled the delicate skin, he rolled her over until she lay spread over his body, impaled on his shaft. One firm arm enfolded her back. His other hand held her hips still as he took her.

Beth couldn't move, constricted by the bands of steel wrapped around her. Everything receded until only he consumed her. In that moment, she turned herself over to his keeping, trusting him with her body. Her hips slapped against his as he pulled her head down for a ravenous kiss. She thrust her tongue into his mouth, demanding he match her intensity. Beth ground against him, her hand fisted in his hair, her mouth eating hungrily at his. One hand clawed at his side as her body rushed for the rapture.

She bucked wildly against him. Each rock of her body took her higher still until she fell over the precipice. The orgasm rolled through her body in endless waves of ecstasy. She rode each one to its crest as her inner muscles pulsed. The soft mewing sound from the back of her throat called to him, begging him to join her on her plane of ecstasy.

Azrael could do no other than answer the call. His hips rutted wildly against her. Pushing deep, seating himself to the hilt with each thrust. He allowed her core to milk his climax from him. His head flew back as if the pleasure was unparalleled.

His movement slowed, eventually coming to a stop while the couple struggled to breathe. This had been an amazing demonstration of their trust in one another, something she wouldn't mind repeating often. Their bodies pulsed with the aftereffects of their lovemaking.

With Azrael still seated within her warmth, Beth braced her weight on her forearms, her locks veiling them from the world, and noted the beaming expression on his face. "Why are you smiling?"

"What's not to smile about?" He wrapped his arms around her back and a smug grin took his handsome face.

Beth peeled her body off his and stretched out beside him. "Pretty proud of yourself, then? Think you did a good job?"

"If the number of orgasms you had are any indication, I don't think you are going to complain too much."

"Oh, there were things to complain about."

Azrael propped himself up on one elbow. His brows knit down over his eyes. "What do you mean? Are you not satisfied? I can fix that."

His hand trailed down her body heading south. Beth stilled it by lacing her fingers with his. "I'm feeling deliciously sore in all the right places."

"So, what did you mean by 'things to complain about?'"

"My complaint is that we didn't do that sooner."

The relief on Azrael's face made Beth burst out laughing. His own deep answering chuckle filled the space as he settled back on the bed and pulled her into his arms.

"I can't turn back time, but we can certainly do that again in the future, Beth."

"I'd like that." Beth laid her head on his chest and listened to the beat of his heart. "I'd like that a lot."

"There's no time like the present." Azrael rolled on top of her.

Beth shimmered and phased, turning ethereal. Azrael passed right through her. The reaper pushed off the bed like a fire burned beneath him.

*So much for another go-round*, thought Tabetha.

"Sorry," she offered.

Azrael shook his head. "Not your fault."

"I just wish I could control the shifting." Tabetha used her magic to place some ghostly clothes on her body.

Azrael ran a hand through his black hair. "Me too. Maybe soon, once Legba aids us in unraveling who did this to you."

Beth gave him a sad smile. "Yeah. Sure. Maybe then."

Azrael placed his hand next to where her cheek should have been and waited for Beth to meet his sorrowful gaze. "Keep hope. We will figure this out. And in the meantime, we will take advantage of every second you are corporeal."

Hope blossomed in her chest. "I never would have thought the Grim Reaper would be so optimistic."

Azrael grinned. "I have layers."

"Like an onion?"

"More like a cinnamon roll."

"Mmmmmm. I love cinnamon rolls." Beth licked her lips. Azrael tracked the movement with his eyes.

"Oh, you do, do you? Well, maybe the next time you are solid, you can try my roll." Azrael wagged his dark eyebrows, and a silly, lopsided grin took his sexy lips.

One of Beth's brows shot up in return. "Promise?"

"Oh yeah, baby. That's one promise I plan on keeping."

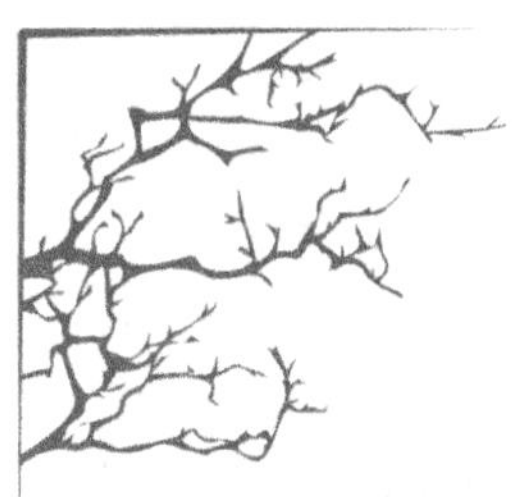

# Chapter 7

Azrael wiped the sleep from his eyes as his brain came back online. Stretching his legs and arms in opposite directions, a sigh of contentment escaped his lips. He reached a hand over beside him ready to rub his sweetheart awake. Shock of an empty bed registered, and he rolled to find a vast emptiness that left him bereft.

"I hate waking up without Beth," Azrael murmured. "I wonder where she went."

He pushed from the bed. The cool air against his naked form shocked the last of the cobwebs from his mind. She loved playing games, especially hide-and-seek that ended in them tumbling into each other's arms. Perhaps she lay waiting for him to discover her hiding place.

He glanced about the spacious bedroom, searching for any sign of his beloved. The dark walls with their gothic style dressing and floor-to-ceiling arched windows were the perfect complement to his dark mahogany dresser. He crossed the room to the matching armoire and threw open the doors wide.

"Not in there," Azrael commented, closing the door. "But seeing my clothes hanging there reminds me."

He glanced down at his nakedness, and with a snap, clothing appeared.

"That's better. Now back to our little game of hide-and-seek."

The rumpled bed, large enough for them to lie widthwise and still not reach the sides, stood proudly against the opposite wall. Perhaps she was under it? A wide grin lifted the corners of his mouth.

Azrael tiptoed across the faux fur carpet, bent down, and snatched the black dust ruffle as high as he could. Pitch dark met his eyes. With a snap, he sent light flooding the space. Disappointment snatched the smile from his face when nothing but a few dust bunnies greeted him.

Dropping the material, he stood. "Okay, so she isn't under here."

He listened carefully for any noise to indicate where he might find her. A deafening silence filled the room. Had something happened?

For months, they had awakened together in his bed each day. Heck, most days had begun with a rousing round of making whoopie. In fact, now that he thought about it, this was the first time he'd awakened to discover her gone.

Panic rose, bile in his stomach coming along for the ride. A thick swallow forced it from making an appearance. Had something happened to Beth? Lately, she remained corporeal for longer periods of time, but eventually still turned into a ghostly form. But even when in spirit form, he could always see her. What if that had changed?

Or worse, what if she was gone?

Azrael's heart raced. They just assumed she would remain with him, at least until he reaped her soul once it could rest in peace. But what if...no, it was too painful to even consider.

But the thought wouldn't leave his brain. It wiggled and writhed until he silently voiced the unimaginable. *What if another reaper had discovered her and taken her while she was in ethereal form?* Anything might happen if she became corporeal in the afterlife. Such a thing had never happened before. No one, including Azrael, knew what the consequences of such a thing might be.

Fear propelled him forward. He raced through each room upstairs. She wasn't anywhere.

He beat bare feet down the stairs. Was she in the living room?

No.

In the parlor?

No!

In the game room?

No!!

"Tabetha!" He screamed her name to the heavens.

"In here," the sweetest voice he'd ever heard called from the kitchen.

Hope made him break into a run. When he threw open the door, the best sight in the world greeted him.

Tabetha stood in front of the stove, an apron tied around her tiny waist. When she registered that he'd entered, she turned in his direction, a skillet in one hand and a spatula in the other.

The grin on her face widened when their eyes met. Relief flooded his body. She was okay. Better than okay, she was corporeal, flesh and bone.

"Are you hungry?" she asked. "I made breakfast."

Azrael crossed the room in four long strides. Taking the pan and utensil from her grasp, he laid them on the stove and took her in his arms. "You scared me to death. I woke up and couldn't find you."

Her hands found his biceps as she smiled before she replied. "Scared to death? I wouldn't think that would be an issue for the Grim Reaper."

Azrael's left eyebrow shot up in disbelief. She joked? About something so serious? Did she not understand the depth of his feelings?

Well, he knew how to fix that.

"Beth, do you have any idea how much I have come to care for you?"

"Azrael, we've talked about this. We have no idea what the future holds for us."

The reaper shook his head. "I don't care. I will do whatever it takes for us to be together. Don't you have feelings for me and want to remain here?"

"Of course, I do. I simply meant that we can't be sure what the future will bring."

"I don't care. I don't care if you become permanently ethereal. I don't care if you keep going back and forth between being solid or ghostly."

"I feel the same, although I must admit, I much prefer to be corporeal because we can do things like this."

Beth lifted to her toes. Her hands trailed up his arms, over his shoulders to cradle his jaw. She leaned in. When their lips touched, electricity zinged through his body. Her lips opened in invitation. An invitation he gladly accepted. He deepened the kiss. She tasted of tea and woman, a heady combination. Blood rushed to his most manly part, making it stand ready for action.

Beth giggled when it pressed into her stomach and broke the kiss. "I see you don't exactly hate me being solid either."

She wiggled her eyebrows, making Azrael laugh. "No, I don't. In fact, it wouldn't break my heart if you became permanently corporeal."

"Wouldn't that mean that I'd have to return to the human realm?" Beth's hands dropped from his jaw to return to his forearms.

"I honestly don't know. A human has never lived on this plane. I have no idea if such a thing is possible. But then nothing says you would be human again, even if you were permanently corporeal."

A deep sigh pushed Beth's bosom against his torso in the most delicious way before her form wavered, and she became ghostly once more. "Looks like we can save that discussion for another day."

Azrael's arms dropped to his sides. His body ached from her absence. Even after all these months, it was still an odd sensation to have her against his body, experiencing all the sensations that came with that, and then instantly having her ghost away, leaving him bereft.

The sound of the doorbell pulled him from his musings.

"You better go get that." Beth glided away from him. "Perhaps it's Papa Legba with news finally."

"That would be nice for a change. I'm tired of his updates not having anything of substance to them."

As Azrael made his way through the home to the foyer, he sent a silent prayer out to whatever god or goddess might be listening to have Legba at the door with some good news.

Azrael opened the door wide. And the sight greeting him made him apprehensive and hopeful at the same time.

"Legba," he greeted with a handshake. "Welcome. Do you have news?"

"May I come in?"

As the male pushed through the door, Azrael's trepidation grew, not from the eternal ashen makeup that made the top half of Legba's face seem skeletal, but from the fear that they might never figure out who killed his Beth.

Azrael made a sweeping gesture with his arm toward the living room. "Let's have a seat so we can talk."

Legba nodded curtly and quick-timed it through the foyer and into the living room like a man on a mission. Rather than sit, he chose to stand next to one of the bookshelves. He fingered one of the leather-bound books on the shelf, the gesture made him appear absent-minded, but Azrael knew better. This male never did anything without a purpose. The reaper sat in his favorite chair and placed a hand on each knee, then waited for the other male in the room to speak.

Legba cleared his throat just as Tabetha glided through the entryway. "Papa Legba, I'm so glad to see you."

"And I you, *cher*. 'Tis good to lay eyes on ya." His pinched face gave a tiny nod before a slight smile lifted the corners of his mouth.

Beth returned the grin. "Did you come bearing news? Have you learned who killed me?"

If Azrael had blinked, he would have missed the shudder that coursed through Legba before he spoke. "As you know, I have been having...pillow talk with Miss Hestaba."

If Tabetha were not in the room, Azrael would have pressed for details. Not many immortals got to mix parts with humans. He couldn't help but wonder if it differed from being with an immortal. Gods knew that being with Tabetha was as close to nirvana as he'd ever been. He wondered if that was because of her soul's condition or whether it was due to the feelings he'd developed for her.

Legba's hand dropped to his side, and he paced back and forth in front of the fireplace. "I have gotten to know her well these past months, more than any other human in all my long lifetime. And yet, there was a part of her she kept hidden from me. Until last night."

"Please go on," Beth prompted, gliding to stand next to Azrael.

He wished he could reach out and grab her hand as they awaited Legba's news. His irritation mounted. Irritation at her condition, irritation at waiting for the news. "Legba, out with it. Please!"

Legba stopped and turned to face the couple. "For months I tried to get da witch to talk of your death, Tabetha. Last night she finally did."

"What did she say?" Tabetha prompted, her eyes wide.

"Hestaba believes Bella had a hand in your demise. Said someting about you and Bella having a history. She also mentioned dat there is to be a séance tonight, and she referenced the one last year when the coven asked me to bless them. She claimed Alli told her you and Bella argued after the séance."

Tabetha nodded. "I wouldn't exactly call it an argument, but she was snippy."

"Luckily, Hestaba asked me to bless the coven again on this Halloween, said they would summon me during tonight's séance. I asked her if Bella would be in attendance, and she said, 'absolutely she would.' I see dis as a chance for me to have time with this Bella. Since Hestaba believes 'tis Bella who killed you, I can demand she take Hestaba's place as sacrifice, if you know what I imply."

Azrael clapped his hands as a joyful warmth spread throughout his body. "That is brilliant! If you can get her alone, you can extract a confession from her."

An evil grin lit Legba's brown eyes. "Exactly. One way or another, I'll get her to confess tonight."

"We should be there too," Azrael suggested.

"We?" Beth didn't keep the shock from her tone. "Is that even possible? Can I go to the human plane?"

Azrael shrugged. "I'm not sure. What do you think, Legba?"

Legba fisted his hands on his hips. "If anyone can do it, Tabetha can. In a way, she walks both worlds. If she follows you, Azrael, she should be able to cross over."

"Like Father Time does when we reap a soul?" Azrael's statement came out as a question.

Legba nodded, his top hat bobbing with his head as his long, thin braids fell over his shoulders. "Exactly. Whatever you do to transport others to the human realm should work on Tabetha I tink. Hurry now. The pull of the summoning is upon me. I must go."

With a nod of his head, Legba's form faded and coalesced into itself before disappearing entirely.

*With Beth already in ghostly form, traveling between realms should be easy*, thought Azrael. He rose and, with a snap, used his powers to change his clothing into the traditional reaping outfit of dark, leather pants, black tee-shirt, and leather duster.

Beth's eyes roamed his body, from his shit-kicker boots up to his carefree black hair. She chewed her lower lip between her teeth and eyed him in a way that made him want to carry her upstairs. "Damn, you are so sexy when you dress for reaping."

"Glad you think so." He wagged his black brows. "You are sexy no matter what or how little you have on. I just wish you were corporeal, so I could show you just how sexy you are."

"There will be plenty of time for that later. Right now, I believe we have a séance to get to."

An exasperated sigh blew through Azrael's lips. "Fine. But I will hold you to your offer of sexy time later."

Beth giggled. "You better."

"All right, touch my arm. I'll use my power to take us to the mortal realm."

As Tabetha's fingers alighted on his forearm, Azrael closed his eyes in concentration. Finding the house with the séance would be a little difficult given that he usually followed the thread of the dying to get to the human plane. He decided to focus his mind on Papa Legba. Finding his thread, he pulled his form inward, melding his essence with Tabetha's to take her along for the ride and hoped for the best.

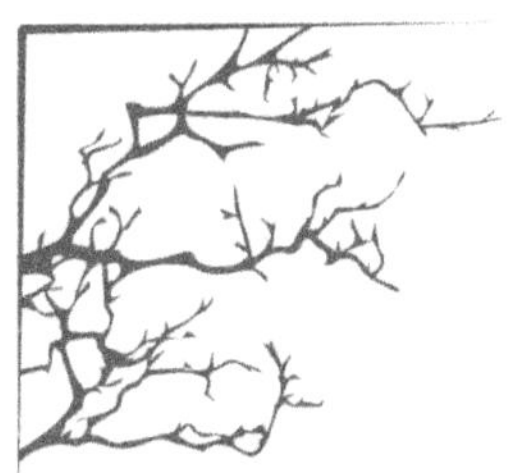

# Chapter 8

Tabetha's vision cleared as she and Azrael reconstituted. An unnerving sense of familiarity washed over her as she took in the sight. They stood in Alli's home. The same home where just a year before, she had participated in a séance that kicked off a series of events that changed her life in ways unimaginable.

Nothing had changed since the year prior. Well, nothing except Beth herself and Azrael, of course. She locked eyes with her lover. It was bizarre to see through him.

"I'm in reaper form," he stated in answer to her unasked question. "We want to stay incognito. Let's just observe the activities. Maybe we'll learn something before Legba does."

Tabetha nodded. "Look!" she whispered. "It's Hestaba."

"You don't need to whisper. They can't hear or see us," Azrael explained as Tabetha scanned the room.

Tonight, just as the previous Halloween, the living room had been transformed. Dark curtains, in shades of maroon and black, again draped the bookcases full of old tomes. With the furniture removed, only the carpet with a large Hecate's wheel symbol lay on the hardwood floor. The grouping of candles, encircled by rows of pillows, cast a soft, yellow-orange glow about the room.

Papa Legba had arrived before them and now stood in the center of the grouping. He turned in a slow circle before addressing Hestaba.

"What do you wish of me, woman, on dis most sacred of nights?"

Hestaba shook out her shoulder-length blonde hair. There wasn't a wrinkle on her face, and Tabetha couldn't help but wonder if she possibly did a little magic to keep herself looking so youthful.

"I wish to have your blessing for my coven," Hestaba's voice rang out like a good leader's should, compelling and steady. "We will be participating in the competition again this year. We seek your blessing upon us so that we may win again and solidify our rightful place as the most powerful coven in the region."

Papa Legba moved with a gracefulness Beth had never noticed before. He seemed to glide on air until he came to rest directly in front of Hestaba. He knelt so they met eye to eye. "And what will you give me as payment for my blessing?"

Hestaba's eyes lowered, and she bowed her head. "I humbly offer myself."

Legba threw back his head and a low, hardy laugh burst forth that created cracks in his ashen makeup. "You? I've had *you* for the past year."

As he stood to his full height, Hestaba's face contorted into a sneer of disbelief. Legba's pallid eyebrow shot up on his forehead as if to dare her to challenge him.

Hestaba seemed to gather her wits. A blank expression painted her face. Her chest rose slowly before falling, indicating she'd taken a deep, no doubt calming breath. "If not me, then what do you have in mind as payment?"

Papa Legba turned a slow circle. "I tink..." he gave a slow perusal of the group, "I tink she will do."

Legba pointed at Belladonna.

"Me?" Bella's eyes widened.

"Her?" Hestaba's eyes narrowed in disbelief.

"Her," Legba replied simply, his tone booked no argument. "If you wish my blessing, it will be given only after I spend a bit of time alone with her."

Hestaba's jaw ticked. "Where would you like to have this alone time?"

"We shall make use of a bedroom here." Legba crossed the circle and held out his hand to Bella.

The witch reluctantly placed her hand in his and allowed him to pull her to her feet. "Now if someone would be so kind as to show us to somewhere private."

Alli dropped the hands she held and rose. "I-I will show you to my room if that will be acceptable."

Legba grabbed the brim of his top hat and bowed deep at the waist. "Lead the way."

Alli proceeded the couple down the hall. Beth and Azrael followed in tow.

"I'm not sure I want to see this," Beth remarked.

"Oh, I believe you might." Azrael's grin made his eyes crinkle. "Legba is a great interrogator. You don't want to miss this."

Beth noted the photos hanging in the hall as they made their way through. Each one a memory that she shared with the family who had adopted her after her parents died. No way Alli would have betrayed her.

When they arrived at the bedroom decked out in various shades of pastels, Alli held the door for the couple. It was Legba who spoke first.

"Tank you, *cher*. We shan't be needing any more of your time dis night."

Alli appeared almost relieved. "Of course. As you wish, Papa Legba."

When Alli closed the couple in the room, Legba marched Bella into a wooden chair next to a lamp with a shawl draped over the shade. The surprise on her face raised her brows into her bangs. Her mouth gaped open.

"I can see you are confused," Legba began. He shrugged out of his coat and rolled up his sleeves while he continued. "Let me explain. I am friends with Tabetha. And she and Azrael—"

"Who is Azrael?" Bella's confusion made her hands fist in her lap.

"He is a good friend of mine...and of Tabetha's. In fact, he is the reason I chose you. See, Tabetha and Azrael need answers, and you, *cher,* are going to provide them."

"Answers about what?" Belladonna squirmed in the wooden chair.

"Answers about who killed Tabetha." Papa Legba moved in front of Bella. "And you are going to give them to me."

"I have no idea what you are talking about."

"Oh, I tink you do." Legba moved a little closer. "Who killed Tabetha?"

"No one."

Legba tsked. "Now, now. A pretty, little witch shouldn't lie. Let's try this again. Someone in your coven killed Tabetha. We tink it was you. Did you kill her?"

Bella's fingers tightened on the arms of the chair as her body retreated against the back of the seat. "I-I do not know what you are talking about."

Papa Legba shrugged and curled his upper lip. "Fine. We do dis the hard way then."

Legba reached out his hand. The second it touched Bella's forehead, her neck snapped back, and a blood-curdling scream filled the room. Bella's face distorted in pain. Tabetha's stomach churned at the sight.

"What is he doing?" Tabetha asked Azrael.

"He's pulling the information from her mind."

"My goddess. Why didn't he give her more chances to answer his questions?"

"Legba doesn't like to waste time," Azrael supplied, as if that excused his behavior.

Before Beth could reply, Alli burst through the door, the entire coven on her heels. "What the hell is going on? Take your hand off Bella. Now!"

To Tabetha's surprise, Papa Legba did just that. The Vodou God turned to face the group. "We need to talk, Alli." His gaze flew to the group of women behind her. "In private."

He flung a hand in their direction. The entire coven, save Tabetha's best friend, was flung from the door of the room. They landed in the hall with a collective hump. As they began to murmur, Legba twisted his wrist, slamming the door shut and locking it with his powers.

"Now," his voice calm and steady. "Let's talk. But first, I'm going to need Azrael and Beth to join us."

Legba snapped his fingers. Her friend recoiled in fear and shock as Beth and Azrael became visible.

Alli's hand flew to her mouth. "Y-you—you're dead."

"You should know," Legba said. "After all, you killed her."

Shock sent electricity down Tabetha's spine. The world threatened to spin. Her knees, though still ethereal, felt weak.

Azrael's form solidified. Anger flushed his face. His eyes narrowed on Alli. She wisely backed away.

"I-I didn't kill her."

"You lie, witch." Legba rolled down his sleeves and buttoned them before continuing.

"She wouldn't lie," Tabetha pleaded, shaking her head fervently. "She is like a sister to me. She'd never betray me, let alone kill me."

Papa Legba's eyes softened when they landed on Tabetha. "I am truly sorry to be da one to break da news, but I found it all in Belladonna's mind. There is no doubt it was her that did you in."

"Tell me what you saw." Disdain dripped from Azrael's voice. The muscle along his jaw flinched. "I need to know everything."

Alli turned and grabbed the door. She twisted the nob with both hands. The thing looked like it might break under the pressure, and Beth was afraid she would make a run for it. But Legba had other plans.

"Come here," he commanded and extended an arm in her direction.

The witch's body stilled. Her hands dropped to her side, and she turned robotically from the door. With stiff legs, she marched across the room. When she arrived beside Bella, she sat awkwardly on the floor next to her chair. Beth noticed Belladonna for the first time since all hell had broken loose.

The young witch remained slumped in the chair, her neck resting on the wooden back in an unnatural position. Her lips, blue in color, were wide as if gasping for air. Her eyes stared sightlessly at the ceiling. Relief flooded Beth when she noticed Bella's chest rise and fall. She lived.

At least for now.

"Do you want to tell him what you did, or shall I?" Legba asked Alli.

"Release me from your binding magic," Tabetha's friend spit out through a clenched jaw.

Legba smiled. "So, you can work your magic? I don't tink so. Now tell Azrael what you did to poor Tabetha."

"I will not!" the ever-defiant Alli ground out.

Disbelief bubbled her blood until Tabetha shook with the effort to contain it. "Tell him, Alli. You don't want to end up like Bella."

Her friend's gaze gave Bella's frozen form a once-over. Fear, or maybe repulsion, widened her eyes.

Papa Legba crossed his arms over his chest. "You see, bad tings happen to those who don't cooperate. You know my power. Do you really tink to defy me?"

"Someone better tell me what she did to Beth and now," Azrael roared.

Clearly, his patience had reached its limits just as Tabetha's had.

When her former friend didn't volunteer an explanation, Legba shrugged and rolled his eyes. 'Stubborn witch. Guess I will have to share da story. Our little Alli here is the one who killed Tabetha. She poisoned her."

Tabetha moved closer. "How? She wasn't anywhere near my home when I died."

"She didn't have to be. Apparently, she knew you were going to be coming into the apothecary."

Tabetha gasped. Her hand flew to her mouth before she spoke. "I remember now. I had run into her the day before at the coffee shop. I mentioned that I wanted to practice making my grandmother's healing potion, but I needed to get more Dittany of Crete Leaf."

Legba turned toward Beth. "She got there before you and poisoned the leaves with a spell. After you bought the leaves, she reversed the spell before they could kill anyone else. Bella saw da whole ting, but it wasn't 'til you die dat she put it all together."

"Why?" Beth knelt before Alli to look her in the eye. "Why would you do that to me? I've always been a good friend. I loved you like a sister."

Hate narrowed Alli's eyes. Spittle flew from her mouth when she spoke. "Why? Why? You know why."

Beth shook her head. "I have no idea."

"Oh, come on. You were going to usurp me, take over as leader of the coven when Hestaba stepped down. I couldn't let that happen."

"What are you talking about? I wasn't going to take over as leader. I would never do that to you."

"She overheard a few of the coven members talking about how powerful you are," Legba supplied. "When you summoned me to the séance last year, Alli felt your power and realized it was far superior to her own. She decided to kill you and remove the threat before you became too powerful to stop."

"Is that true?" Azrael asked. "You really killed Tabetha simply because you thought she would replace you as coven leader one day?"

"You don't understand. It wasn't that simple. When Tabetha came to live with us, my parents gave her everything. All their attention. All their love. Everything changed the minute she came into our lives. I was no longer the special one. I was no longer the most powerful one. I was no longer the one who was most loved." A tear rolled down Alli's cheek. "Being the coven leader is all I've ever wanted, because I'd finally be loved and respected. The thought of her taking that from me like she'd taken my parents' love...that injustice couldn't be allowed to happen, so I made sure it didn't."

"You took her life for nothing!" Azrael screamed. "Nothing!"

The reaper trembled. His eyes blazed with white-hot anger. The next moment time slowed in a way only possible during great danger. The grim raced forward. One hand pinned Alli to the floor. Her eyes bulged from their socket. Capillaries burst, turning her eyes red. Her fingers futilely scratched at Azrael's skin, but his grip only tightened. Alli's magic leapt to her defense, energy sparked from her fingertips. She aimed all ten digits toward Azrael.

Tabatha screamed.

It spurred Azrael into action.

Before Alli could release her sorcery, Azrael used his free hand to send an invisible blade of magic across her throat. The skin opened wide; a red river flowed from the opening. Pain mixed with shock to distort Alli's face. Her mouth opened and closed in a soundless scream before a gurgle escaped the seeping wound. Her eyes faded from violet to white. As she took her last breath, Azrael reached into her chest and yanked the soul from her corpse. It struggled against his hold, flailing like a cloth caught in a whipping wind. The reaper tightened his grip and pulled it to him, so they were close enough for her to feel his breath when he spoke.

"I'm taking you to the afterlife you deserve for killing Beth."

"Noooooooooooo!" Alli's scream died as their forms coalesced into nothingness.

Legba's dark eyes flew to Tabetha just as her mouth gaped over.

"Well, I didn't see dat coming. How about you?" asked Legba with a cocky grin.

Tabatha stood and shook her head slowly, surprise keeping her mute.

"Okay then. I guess dat settles things. We not only discovered who killed you, but justice has been served. That wraps tings up nice and neat." Papa Legba wiped his hands on one another in a that-is-that gesture. "You feel at peace now?"

Did she? If Tabetha were honest with herself, she felt numb. The kind of numb you experienced when shock mixed with awe. Everything had happened so fast. No time to process. She blinked at Legba. He looked at her expectantly, like a child waiting for an at-a-boy. She couldn't help but want to please him, to reassure him.

Beth's head nodded of its own volition.

"Excellent. With Azrael busy dealing with your sister-friend, 'tis only fair dat I help him out, don't you tink?"

Beth absently nodded for a second time.

Legba showed his perfect teeth with a wide grin. "Good. But first, I need to finish up here."

Legba snapped his fingers. Bella's body rose from the chair and floated onto the bed.

His attention returned to Tabetha. "Now, we can't have anyone seeing you."

The god snapped his fingers a second time. Before Beth could confirm she was once again invisible, he turned toward the door and with a twist of his hand it opened.

"Hestaba," he called. "Would you come here a minute?"

The coven leader peeked her head in the door.

"There you are, *cher*. Bella needs your help. She will need a healing spell performed on her mind. Can you and your coven take care of dat for me?"

Hestaba's gaze fell to poor Bella. Repulsion distorted her features when she registered the condition of her fellow coven member.

"Wh-what happened to her?" Hestaba placed her hand over her heart.

"Dat can wait for another time. As you can see Alli is gone." Legba gestured toward her body. Hestaba's eyes tracked the movement and widened in understanding. "You will need to do someting about her as well."

"What happened to—"

"Do keep up, *mon cher*. I don't have time to be repeating." Legba crossed the room in three powerful steps, took Hestaba's hand, and pulled her into the room. "Alli is dead. And you need to perform a healing spell on Belladonna's mind, or she will remain in a coma for the rest of her days. You understand?"

Hestaba nodded. "I understand."

"Good, good." Papa Legba retrieved his jacket from the bed, shrugged into the dark coat, and gave the lapels a tug. "Now as an added bonus for all the trouble tonight, I give your coven my blessing. You see, Tabetha has become rather special to me, and I want to help her coven recover."

"Tabetha? Our Tabetha?"

"She isn't yours anymore, but yes. The same Tabetha who was a member of your coven."

Hestaba lowered her head, tears flowing down her cheeks. For the first time Tabetha could remember, the coven priestess showed a moment of weakness. The sight broke Tabetha's heart. Desperate to comfort her leader, Tabetha moved beside Hestaba and willed the witch to see her.

Alas, she did not. Tabetha swallowed the lump in her throat as she extended an ethereal arm in comfort the woman couldn't feel. Sadness pushed a tear from Beth's eye. It flowed down her cheek. When it hit the floor, it seemed to signal Legba into action.

"All right now. Enough of dis sadness. Time to dry your tears. There is much to celebrate. Tabetha can finally rest in peace."

Hestaba's head jerked up. "What do you mean?"

"Oh, nothing. A last word of advice before I go. Hestaba, be the strong witch I know you are and do right by your coven. They have lost much."

Hestaba squared her shoulders. After wiping the tears from her face, she vowed, "I will."

With that, Legba turned ethereal and faded from Hestaba's sight. He turned to Tabetha and took her hand in his. It was strange to feel in this ghostly form, but, for some reason, with Legba she could.

"Let's go. The least I can do is escort you to the afterlife."

"Wait! What about Azrael?"

"What about him? He's busy, and now that you are at peace, you should be able to enter the afterlife. Ready?"

"Not really."

Legba gave a hollow chuckle. "No one ever is, *cher.*"

Legba snapped his fingers, and Beth's form coalesced into nothingness.

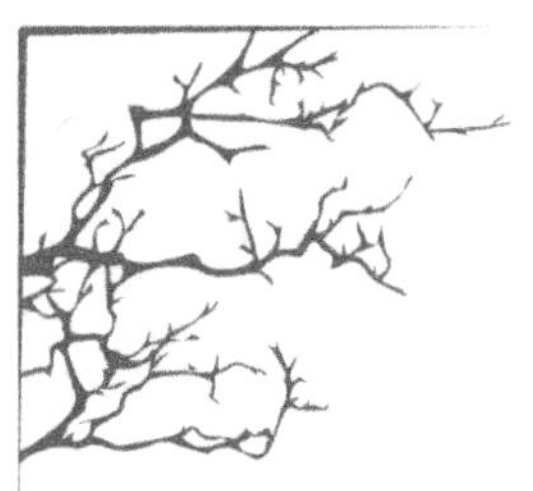

# Chapter 9

Azrael materialized in his home. Satisfaction and pride oozed from every pore. He'd not only doled out judgement to the monster who had killed his Beth, but he'd personally seen to it that Alli's disgusting, evil soul had gone to an afterlife that would guarantee torture for eternity. A wide grin lifted the corners of his mouth to his ears at the memory of the expression on the witch's face when she discovered such a thing existed as Hell for witches, no matter what their beliefs might otherwise imply. He couldn't wait to share the news with Beth. Heck, forget that. He couldn't wait to see her, touch her, celebrate with her.

"Beth," he called. "Beth, love, I'm home. Where are you?"

Anticipation of holding his love spurring him on, he took the stairs two at a time. He cleared each room on the second floor like a secret agent, swift and thorough, but Tabetha was nowhere to be found. Trepidation and disappointment slammed into him with the one-two punch of a prizefighter, twisting his gut. Sadness pushed in, the force so great it almost dropped him to his knees. In that moment, his brain finally admitted what it had suppressed for all these months.

He loved her.

The acknowledgment stopped his feet, demanding introspection. He *loved* her. Tabetha brought laughter to his life. She was his everything, his reason for getting up each day. If he spent the rest of his long life making her happy, it would never be long enough. He couldn't wait to see her to declare his love.

He bounded down the curved stairway and made quick work of sweeping through the rest of the home.

"Where is she?" he murmured, swiping a hand through his shaggy, dark hair. "Surely, Legba would have brought her back here by now."

Legba! Of course, she must be with him.

With a thought, Azrael materialized on Legba's front porch. He used the lion's-head knocker to demand entry. Excitement bubbled in his veins. He couldn't wait to hold Beth in his arms and profess his love for her.

The door opened and from within, Legba called, "Come on in, Azrael."

Azrael's long strides took him gracefully through the entry.

Legba joined him in the foyer, his arms wide in greeting. "Welcome. I take it the reaping of Alli went well."

Azrael nodded. "The witch got everything she deserved."

Legba cocked his head and smirked. "I never doubted you would see to it she received an appropriate punishment."

Azrael's gaze took in the room. "Where is Tabetha? I can't wait to see her."

Legba's dark brows united over the bridge of his thick nose. "She is not here."

"What do you mean, she isn't here?" Azrael mimicked Legba's confused look and clenched his hands at his sides. "Where is she? You didn't leave her in the human realm?"

"Do you tink I'm new to the afterlife?" Legba scoffed. "Of course, I didn't leave her soul there. I escorted her to where she can be at peace."

Confusion turned to a deadly combination of fear and anger as Legba's statement sunk in. He wouldn't! He couldn't! There was no way he'd actually reaped Beth. Azrael took a deep, calming breath that did absolutely nothing. His jaw clamped shut.

Dreading the answer, through locked teeth he asked, "Where *exactly* did you take Beth?"

"To purgatory so a reaper could escort her to Summerland."

"What!" Rage flowed through Azrael's veins like fiery lava. "How...why?"

Damn, he couldn't even form a complete sentence. Fury mixed with the fear of never seeing her again in a lethal combination.

Legba smiled. "You don't have to tank me. You were busy dealing with Alli, so I helped you by taking Tabetha as far as I could in her afterlife journey. I apologize for my inability to take her to Summerland, but I'm sure by now another reaper has found her and escorted her there safely."

"You just left her there, by herself?" The incredulousness did not escape Azrael's tone. "How could you!"

Legba straightened the lace cuffs on his shirt. "Her soul found peace. She will be fine once she is reaped."

Legba's casual tone made the irritation build in Azrael until he had difficulty forming his response. "That's not...I meant how could you take her there instead of bringing her here?"

From under his top hat, Legba's eyes met Azrael's. "Why ever would I bring her here?"

"Because she is meant to be with me. I love her."

"You what?" Legba's eyes went wide, and he tilted his head to one side in consideration.

"I love her...And now she is gone...forever."

The weight of despair sent Azrael to his knees. He buried his face in his hands.

Legba placed a hand on Azrael's shoulder and gave it a squeeze. "I'm sorry. I didn't realize you developed such deep feelings for da woman. But you know she was bound to find peace and go to da afterlife at some point, didn't you?"

Azrael shrugged and shook his head as he looked up at his friend. "I thought we had more time to figure that out. I hope..." His voice hitched on the emotion in his throat.

"You had hoped she would be able to remain with you?" Legba supplied.

Azrael nodded. His head slumped on his neck.

Legba moved so he faced Azrael. He grabbed the reaper by the shoulders and pulled him to his feet. "Then go get her."

"I can't. The only way out of purgatory for a soul is to the afterlife, and once there, a soul can never leave. As you said, a reaper has probably already escorted her to Summerland."

Legba gripped each of Azrael's shoulders. "If anyone is powerful enough to pull her from Summerland, 'tis you."

"I can't. It doesn't work that way. Once a soul has reached its final destination there is no return."

"Then mayhap she hasn't been reaped. She may still be in purgatory."

Hope blossomed in Azrael's stomach. It grew to straighten his spine. Legba was correct. He *could* take a soul from purgatory. If, by some miracle, Beth was still there, then maybe just maybe he could find a way to bring her to the immortal realm instead of Summerland. It was a chance.

His only chance.

"You're right. I have to go immediately."

Legba dropped his hands to his sides. "So why you still here?"

Azrael closed his eyes in concentration and found the ethereal thread that led to purgatory. He dematerialized his form into atomic particles and glided along the thread until it stopped. He reformed in the gray landscape.

His discerning gaze took in every nuance. The land stretched out flat as far as the eye could see with only the occasional boulder to mar the scape. An otherworldly fog swirled thickly along the surface. A few spindly trees, their bare branches a perfect perch for the ravens, created monstrous shadows on the fog which oscillated in time with the movement of the mist. In all directions, souls waited. A few of them stood stone-still as if in shock, while others wandered aimlessly through the haze. It turned Azrael's stomach when he realized the horror Beth must have felt looking over the scene.

Never, in all the millenniums he'd brought souls here to await their ultimate fate, had he stopped to consider what being here must be like. With the love of his life possibly still in this nightmare, he now watched the scene with abject horror. The thought of her being in this place, with no color or happiness, made bile rise, and his last meal threatened to make an appearance.

He must find her.

"Beth!" He moved forward through the fog and cupped his hands around his mouth. "Tabetha, are you here?"

A few of the souls turned his way, but none answered.

And none were his Beth.

He ran forward for an eternity, all the while scanning every soul and calling to his love. Each time silence met his call, or the wrong face turned his way. Each disappointment nicked his heart until it bore one thousand lashes. Azrael stumbled from the pain. Maybe he was too late. Maybe she'd been taken to Summerland.

THE HARD, POINTY BOLDER pushed into Tabetha's tender skin. She'd been standing for so long, sitting felt good, even if it was on an uncomfortable surface. Cold seeped into her bones, though whether from the actual temperature or the horror of her surroundings, she couldn't be sure. Everywhere she looked, gray, bleak scenery swayed with silent screams. Even the mountains in the distant appeared in shades of gray and black.

Her only real companions? The ravens that clung to the skeletal branches. Their calls carried on the still air, the only sound in this place despite the fact numerous other souls were scattered about.

But the souls refused to talk to her. Heck, they refused to even *acknowledge* her. Oh, Beth had tried talking to enough of them, but alas, they ignored her completely, which would have been all right except time moved differently here. While in her ethereal form, time seemed non-existent. She'd experience awareness of where she was and of waiting for her final reward, but minutes blended into hours or possibly even days for all she knew, and it didn't bother her in the slightest. But the second her body solidified, everything changed.

Each second now ticked by like an eternity. Every moment lasted an epoch. Every blink, each labored breath, every beat of her heart registered in her brain. Instinctually, she knew no one should be corporeal in this place, but she couldn't control it. Oh, she'd tried. She tried with all her might to phase back into her ghostly form, but she couldn't.

A raven circled her head, the beat of its wide wings fluttered her hair as it landed next to her. It cranked its head to the side and peered up at her with one eye.

"Hello, friend." Beth kept her tone intentionally soft and quiet. "Nice of you to drop by...literally"

Beth chuckled. After a lifetime in this bleak place, it was nice to have a fun interaction, even if it was with something that didn't speak. Instinct made Beth reach out to stroke its sleek black feathers.

The raven squawked and took flight, leaving Beth once more to her desolate solitude. She wrapped her arms about her waist. Tears flowed down her face in twin rivers. She couldn't survive an eternity of this. She'd rather be anywhere but here. Desperation took the last of her strength, and she bent at the waist. The mist rose to cover her face, making it hard to breathe. She coughed just as a muffled sound reached her ears.

Was that a yell? Could it be a soul that might finally speak with her to help pass the time? Hope straightened her spine.

"Beth? Is that you, Beth?" a familiar voice called.

Tabetha's head snapped to the left. She squinted her eyes, trying to bring the shadowy form into focus. She rose from the bolder.

"Tabetha?" a deep voice boomed across the sea of fog.

She recognized that voice, loved that voice. Optimism bubbled in her veins.

"Azrael?" Excitement made her limbs tingle.

Happiness, unlike any she'd experienced before, infused her with strength. Her feet moved of their own volition in his direction. Their bodies came together in a crash of energy. Relief coursed through her as it registered his hard form against her soft one. Her arms circled his neck at the exact time his went around her waist. Azrael lifted her from the ground, their lips locking in an emotion-filled kiss. She tasted his desperation to find her, his happiness at having her in his arms. His emotions mixed with hers, feeding hers. Like a circuit of electricity, their feelings flowed between them in a way only possible in a realm such as this. It built with each pass until her brain finally acknowledged what she'd been feeling for months.

Love.

She loved him with all her being and soul.

Unable to contain her emotions, she broke the kiss needing to profess her feelings.

"I love you." They gushed simultaneously.

Their eyes widened in unison before they both let out a giggle.

Azrael pulled her back against him, cradling her head against his muscular chest. The leather duster he wore felt cool against her cheek, but she didn't care. All that mattered was that he loved her.

He ran his fingers through her golden waves, and she settled against him. Tabetha believed with all her heart he would protect her. He would find a way to get her out of here. He had to.

"I thought you'd gone to Summerland," he muttered into the top of her head. "You scared me to death."

"*You* were scared." A chill raced down her spine. "You should try being here for what seemed like an eternity. It was petrifying not knowing how long I'd be here."

Azrael breathed in a deep sigh. "I'm sure it was. Let's get you out of here."

Beth pulled back to meet his eyes. "You can do that? You can get me out of here?"

Azrael nodded. "Of course, but you need to phase back into your ghostly form."

"I've tried, but I can't."

"I may be able to help. Alli tried to bargain with me to get out of her punishment, so I took advantage of her desperation." A smug expression crossed Azrael's features. "I asked her if she was aware of a spell to control your phasing between being corporeal and ethereal."

"Let me guess, she said no."

"Actually, she claimed she did. She recited a spell that, according to her, should let you shift between forms at will."

Hope filled Tabetha's chest. "My goddess! Tell me what it is so we can get out of this dreadful place.

"Grant me the veil of the unseen, like night. To pass through the realms, ethereal and light."

Beth repeated the spell, "Grant me the veil of the unseen, like night. To pass through the realms, ethereal and light."

Disappointment twisted her gut as she flipped her solid hands over in front of her face.

"You may need to concentrate more," Azrael suggested. "Some magic requires deep concentration."

"True. Or perhaps, I need to imagine myself becoming ethereal before I cast the spell."

Tabetha closed her eyes. She visualized herself moving through the air, effortlessly gliding like a wisp of smoke. Her consciousness expanded, connecting with the elements. The whispering wind, the quiet hum of the universe filled her being. Her magic pooled in her chest until it burned.

Tabetha once more whispered the spell, "Grant me the veil of the unseen, like night. To pass through the realms, ethereal and light."

A surge of magic coursed through her. The buzzing in her blood forced her eyes open. Tabetha's form wavered and dissolved. As she became translucent, a sensation of weightlessness and freedom coursed through her. She'd done it! She'd controlled the shifting.

Tabetha bounced up and down. "I did it. I did it!"

The pride on Azrael's handsome features made his eyes sparkle. "I see that. Congratulations, but we should save the celebration until we get out of here."

Beth nodded her agreement. "I can't wait to leave this awful place. But where will we go? Are you taking me to Summerland?"

"No. I believe we better go back to the immortal realm. When we get to my place, we will figure out what to do from there. I just need to get you someplace safe so I can think."

"Your place sounds great to me."

Tabetha placed a hand on the reaper's forearm and closed her eyes. Their forms melded in what was now a familiar and comforting way.

"You can open your eyes. We're back."

When Beth's eyes adjusted to the soft moonlight coming through the large windows, she found herself standing next to Azrael in the foyer of his home. Never had the staircase looked so welcoming.

Azrael smiled down on her ghostly face. Peace flooded Beth's body. She realized she was home. This place, this male was her home.

"I don't ever want to leave here again," she declared.

"I don't ever want you to leave here," he assured her. "I have no idea what the future may hold, but whatever it is, we shall face it together."

"Face it? Is there something I should be aware of?"

Worry drew his brows down deep over his black eyes. "I'll never let anything happen to you or anyone take you from me."

Determination, so intense it seemed almost dangerous, darkened Azrael's gaze. And yet Tabetha knew she was safe with him.

A loud knock startled them both. Azrael moved in front of Beth and opened the door.

"Oh, Legba, it's you." Azrael blew a sigh of relief.

Papa Legba glided through the door, holding a parchment in his hand. "I have someting for you."

Curiosity tilted Beth's head. "What's that?"

"While Azrael searched for you, I took da liberty of securing your right to remain on dis plane."

"What? How?" Azrael scrubbed a hand down his face.

"I met with the Council of Immortals on your behalf. Let's just say, I was able to...influence them into seeing why Tabetha is powerful enough to be here."

Beth's form solidified, and she clapped her hands in joy.

"See what I mean? She is the only soul any of us has ever heard of dat can become corporeal. In fact, she is the most powerful witch I have ever had the pleasure of coming across. I swayed the Council it would be a benefit to us all to have her power in dis realm."

"So, they want to use her?" Azrael placed his body between Beth and Legba. "I'll never allow it."

Papa Legba put a hand up in surrender. "No, no. No one is going to use Tabetha. However, if she desires to use her magic to help us from time to time, well then, dat would be a nice boon for arranging for her to be able to stay, would it not?"

Beth placed a hand on Azrael's bicep and gently turned him to face her. "That is fair. I would do anything to remain here with you. Using my powers from time to time is a small ask."

Azrael shook his head. "You don't know what the Council of Immortals is like, Beth. They will use you, use up all your magic."

"Then you will make sure that doesn't happen. I trust you to keep me safe."

Beth lifted a hand to take Azrael's stray wisps of raven hair from his face and tucked them back against the side of his head. When they fell forward, she laced the dark locks between her fingers and rested her hand on his temple, locking them in place. She looked him deep in the eyes, willing him to see the truth and power behind her next words.

"I was powerful before we met, but with you by my side, I am even more powerful."

Tabetha drew her magic into her heart, collecting it there until it burned from the force. Wanting to surprise her sweetheart, she whispered a spell under her breath and sent her magic out to do her bidding.

Candles appeared on the table and along the windowsills, their yellow light adding to the light from the moon that peaked through the open windows. Red and pink rose petals drifted down from the ceiling in a light rain around the threesome.

Legba cleared his throat. "On dat note, I'm going take my leave." He raised the paper in his hand. "Dis is the official proclamation dat Tabatha is welcome to remain in dis realm. I'll just leave dis here and go. Never let it be said I'm a third wheel."

He placed the parchment down between the candles on the table before making a quick exit.

Beth smiled and wrapped her arms around Azreal's waist. "Papa Legba seemed in a hurry all of a sudden."

Azreal slid his hands up Beth's arms to cup her face. "He sure did. It's almost like he knows."

"Knows what?"

"Knows what I plan on doing to celebrate with you?"

"Oh, and what's that?"

A wicked grin rose one corner of his lips. "I thought you'd never ask."

As Azrael took Beth's mouth in a passionate kiss, her magic lifted them into the air. With rose petals continuing to rain around them, their bodies intertwined and floated in a slow turn while they explored each other thoroughly to celebrate their love, secure in the knowledge they had eternity to love one another.

## Additional Stories by Brenda Sparks

**Stand Alone Novels:**
*A Midsummer's Night Demon*
*Weaver of Dreams*
**Alpha Council Chronicles Series:**
*Alpha Mine*
*Deadly Alpha*
*Alpha Lover*
*Alpha Pair*
*Alpha Revealed*
*Alpha Eternal*
**Holiday Immortal Novella Series:**
*Bewitching the Immortal*
*Immortal Temptation*
*Immortal Fantasy*

## PRAISE FOR BRENDA SPARKS

"Brenda Sparks weaves stories that are filled with sensuality, mystery, drama, and awesome vampire action. They keep you on the edge of your seat and never fail to deliver a satisfying conclusion."
*~DW Adler, author*

"MS. SPARKS TAKES YOU on a journey that'll have you turning pages just to find out what happens."
*~Rhea Regale, author*

"I LOVED THE WORLD BUILDING in (Brenda's) story."
*~Harlie Williams, author*

# About the Author

Brenda Sparks has always loved all things spooky and enjoys incorporating paranormal elements in her writing. She refuses to allow pesky human constraints to get in the way of telling the story. Luckily, the only thing limiting her stories is her imagination. Her characters are strong and courageous, and she adores spending time with them in their imaginary world.

Her idea of a perfect day is one spent in front of a computer with a hot cup of coffee, her fingers flying over the keys to send her characters off on their latest adventure.

Brenda loves to connect with readers. Please visit her online or stop by her website to say hello.

Read more at www.brenda-sparks.com.